Born and raised just outside Toronto, Ontario, **Amy Ruttan** fled the big city to settle down with the country boy of her dreams. After the birth of her second child Amy was lucky enough to realise her lifelong dream of becoming a romance author. When she's not furiously typing away at her computer she's mum to three wonderful children, who use her as a personal taxi and chef.

PREGNANT WITH THE PARAMEDIC'S BABY

AMY RUTTAN

MILLS & BOON

First published in Great Britain 2019
by Mills & Boon, an imprint of HarperCollins*Publishers*
1 London Bridge Street, London, SE1 9GF

Large Print edition 2020

© 2019 Amy Ruttan

ISBN: 978-0-263-08571-6

MIX
Paper from
responsible sources
FSC™ C007454

This book is produced from independently certified FSC™ paper to ensure responsible forest management. For more information visit www.harpercollins.co.uk/green.

Printed and bound in Great Britain
by CPI Group (UK) Ltd, Croydon, CR0 4YY

For my family.
All of them.
Those by blood and those members
I chose.
You mean the world to me.

CHAPTER ONE

OF COURSE. It had to be him.

Dr. Sandra Fraser stood in the ambulance bay of Rolling Creek General Hospital and watched as the most annoying paramedic she'd ever encountered in her years as a trauma surgeon, albeit the sexiest, climbed out of the back of the ambulance, helping his partner bring the gurney down.

Kody Davis was a damn fine paramedic. He was good-looking, and everyone loved him.

Too bad she hated him.

Hate *is a strong word. You don't hate him.*

No, she didn't hate him. He might grate on her nerves and she hated the fact that she was so drawn to him. He wasn't the typical type of man that she'd dated in the past. He was a charmer, everyone loved him, and she made assumptions that he was a playboy.

Of course, that was only an assumption. She didn't know if he was or not, but all the guys that she'd known like him in high school and college, the ones with that same playful, charming, carefree demeanor, had been players. Which was why she steered clear of men like Kody, even if secretly she really was attracted to his type.

She chose men who were sedate and serious.

Yeah, and look where that got you. Divorced and heartbroken.

Still, Kody would be the type to be a playboy. What woman wouldn't be attracted to him? He was tall, at least six foot, and in good shape. He had to be, to be a paramedic. His black hair was always kept neat and he had a gorgeous smile, with a twinkle in his eyes that always made her heart beat just a bit faster.

And then there was his drawl. There was a hint of Southern when he spoke, but she couldn't place what state. He was definitely not from Texas. She couldn't place his accent and it made her wonder where he was from. What his pastimes were. What his favorite food was.

Whether he had a significant other.

She groaned.

Focus.

She wasn't looking for a romantic entanglement. She'd moved to Austin to get away from her heartache. The last thing she needed was some kind of illicit, hot one-night stand with a sexy paramedic who made her heart beat just a little bit faster.

Don't you? Maybe that's exactly what you need.

Sandra shook that thought away. She didn't have time to get annoyed by her thoughts about Kody; she had to put her focus on her patient. She was just annoyed that it was Kody again. That when he was around it made her think about other things. Things she had no wish to think about again.

And since she'd started here at Rolling Hills, she constantly ran into Kody. Didn't he ever take time off?

Why did he always have to be the paramedic that she was assigned to meet?

If she believed in karma or fate or anything like that, she was pretty positive that it was messing with her and really that wasn't fair. She'd already dealt with enough, hadn't she?

"What do we have here, Mr. Davis?" she asked, trying to keep cool and stay impersonal around him.

Kody glanced at her briefly and she saw the small flash of annoyance when she called him Mr. Davis.

He didn't like that formality, she knew that, but it was what Sandra preferred. It kept people out, kept them safely on the other side of her carefully constructed walls.

The last time she'd let someone in, it had broken her heart completely.

It had destroyed her.

She was not going to make that mistake again, even if it meant she didn't really have many friends here in Austin.

"Luke McIver, forty. Passenger in a head-on collision with a cow. Wasn't wearing a seat belt and was ejected through the windshield."

Sandra's eyes widened. "Did you say a cow?"

Kody nodded quickly and then shrugged. "I guess not a cow."

"You guess not a cow?" Sandra asked, confused as she leaned over and examined the patient.

"Well, a longhorn type of cow, but I'm not sure if they're actually a traditional cow."

Sandra shook her head. "They're cows. Texas longhorns."

"Ah. Good to know. I've been wondering. Anyway, the car collided with the longhorn and Mr. McIver wasn't wearing a seat belt. The driver sustained minimum injuries, but Mr. McIver here was eighty over sixty."

Sandra frowned. That was not a good blood pressure reading.

That's low.

And just from looking at the patient, she suspected he had a head trauma, especially since Kody had said the patient was ejected from his seat and went through the windshield. She continued her stabilization of her patient, although Kody had done a good job.

He might try to be too familiar with her, she hated the fact she couldn't stop thinking about him, that she found him interesting and sexy, but she couldn't deny his skills as a paramedic.

Kody Davis went above and beyond in an emergency situation. He could think on his feet, assess and, more importantly, save lives. So she shouldn't complain about having to deal with him. She was lucky he was so good at his work. It made her job that much easier.

"Let's get him into trauma pod three."

"Right, boss lady."

She cringed when he called her boss lady. She *hated* that.

She knew that Kody wasn't using it in a derogatory fashion, but in her experience it was usually used that way. And she detested when people called her that. It reminded her of her shattered life in San Diego.

It reminded her of broken promises and heartache and she knew the only reason he was calling her boss lady was because she called him Mr. Davis. Since they'd met four months ago they were always goading each other.

He always had a smile for her. Always called her boss lady.

That's because he doesn't know you don't like it.

And she didn't tell him because she didn't want any kind of familiarity with him.

Just a professional relationship.

Are you sure?

There was a part of her that wanted more, just to see what it would be like, but she'd been burned by love before. She wasn't going to let that happen again. No matter how much she wanted it to.

Focus.

Kody helped her get the patient into the trauma pod and her residents came in.

Dr. Megan Coombs, the senior resident, immediately took over monitoring the patient's blood pressure. "BP is seventy over fifty."

"We're losing him," Sandra said over the din of residents going about their work. She was glad she didn't have to coddle her residents. They knew what they were doing. She stepped in and began to work her magic. This was the moment when she really shone—this was the kind of moment that she lived for.

Saving a life.

She wasn't going to let Luke McIver die. He might have been foolish not wearing a seat belt, but she was going to save his life.

"I need five hundred ccs of saline stat!" she shouted over the din. She needed to raise his blood pressure so that they could stabilize him and she could find out what was going on inside. As another resident was hooking up the saline, she went over her ABCs of the patient and saw his pupils were still reactive and responsive.

Which was good.

They had a chance to save his life.

"BP is stabilizing," Dr. Coombs said.

"Good." Sandra stepped back. "Dr. Coombs, you can lead this trauma pod. Take the patient for CT scans. Look for a brain bleed and possible internal injuries. Page me when you have the results."

Dr. Coombs nodded. "Yes, Dr. Fraser."

Sandra pulled off her gloves and saw that Kody was still standing in the trauma pod. His blue eyes were fixed on the patient and it was the first time she noticed how stunningly blue his eyes really were.

Her pulse began to race, her blood heating, and she hoped she wasn't blushing as she gazed deep into those eyes.

Get a grip on yourself, Sandra.

"You're still here?" she asked.

Kody smiled, a dimple in his cheek. "You never released me, boss lady."

Sandra rolled her eyes and jammed her yellow trauma gown and gloves into the medical waste bin beside him. "You're excused."

She walked out of the trauma pod, hoping that he didn't follow, but he did.

"Why do you dislike me so much?" he asked.

She stopped in her tracks and turned to face him. "What're you talking about?"

The smile was gone. "I'm good at my job and I have a good rapport with people, but since you arrived at Rolling Creek, you just don't seem to like me much."

She sighed. "I don't dislike you, Mr. Davis. I just prefer to keep things professional at work."

Which was true. She was still trying to heal from the last time she'd let people in. It didn't matter how lonely she was, this was for the best. Her walls were up to protect her heart.

"Ah, so that's why you don't really seem to have any friends," he remarked.

Heat bloomed in her cheeks. "I'm not here to make friends, Mr. Davis. I'm here to save lives."

The twinkle returned to his eyes. "Aren't we all? But it doesn't hurt to put a wee bit of a smile on your face every once in a while. You're looking kind of pinched lately, boss lady."

He tried to move past her, but she blocked his path. "Don't call me that."

"What?" he asked.

"Boss lady. I don't… I don't like it." And she tried to keep her voice from trembling. Kody didn't need to know how her ex-husband had called her something similar when she'd been promoted above him, and after she couldn't get pregnant.

He'd blamed it all on her.

And she'd blamed a lot of her infertility on herself too, but he'd called her boss lady and that brought back too many painful memories. Memories she didn't want to think about or be reminded about here in Austin.

She'd left San Diego four months ago to get away from all that. It had been two years since her divorce was finalized, but it had taken her that long to realize she really needed a fresh start. Austin was where she was born and put up for adoption, it was where her loving adoptive parents had found her, so she'd decided to come back to her roots for her new start.

This was supposed to be her fresh start and she'd learned from her past mistakes. She wasn't going to let anyone in.

So she was half expecting Kody to brush off her concerns, as if they were nothing. It was a harmless name, wasn't it? That was what she'd been told before when she'd told other people she didn't like it.

"Come on, Sandra. We're just joking. Can't you take a joke?"

"I'm sorry," Kody said softly, and she was surprised.

"What?" she asked, not quite believing him.

"I'm sorry that I called you boss lady. If I had known that, I would've never called you that."

"Really?" she asked, surprised.

"Really. I'm sorry, Dr. Fraser."

She didn't know what to say and she was taken aback by his genuine sincerity. No one had ever apologized to her for that before because they all thought the supposed "joke" was harmless, but it hurt her.

"Sure. Of course I really mean it." Kody smiled kindly at her. "You're not the only one who didn't like a nickname given to you as a joke."

Heat bloomed into her cheeks. "I know you don't like to be referred to as Mr. Davis, so I'm sorry for that too."

Kody shook his head. "I don't mind that. That's nothing. Although, it does make me think of my father…but, yeah, I'm no stranger to nicknames that I feel aren't appropriate, nicknames that hurt and are explained away. So, I'm sorry, Dr. Fraser. I hope this won't ruin our working relationship?"

"No. It won't. I appreciate your apology." And she did.

Kody half smiled at her. "Good. I'll see you later."

He walked past her, down the hall toward the ambulance bay.

What just happened?

Something had changed there. He'd got past her walls. Got through her front line of defense and, even though it was the last thing that she'd wanted, she was glad.

Kody stopped and looked back and saw Dr. Fraser walking away. He hadn't meant to hurt her—that was the last thing he'd ever wanted to do when he'd first seen her four months ago. He'd been taken aback by her beauty. Her dark brown hair, always pulled tightly back in a high ponytail, and those dark brown eyes that were keen. She never missed anything. The pink in her high cheekbones that always deepened when she was angry or annoyed or anything.

She hardly smiled. He'd never seen a true smile from her and that was why he always worked so hard to get one, but after a while he'd just thought that she had some pain in her past and he was no stranger to that.

Dr. Sandra Fraser intrigued him. She was a closed book and he wanted to peek inside. Although, he shouldn't.

She was off-limits as far as he was concerned.

She turned and walked in the direction of the radiology floor. Probably because the patient's CT scans were up, and Kody really hoped that the patient pulled through.

This was the only part of his job that he didn't like, because he often didn't know what happened beyond this point. He didn't know what became of the patient.

"You should've become a doctor, then!"

Kody shook his sister Sally's words out of his head.

Yeah, he could've been a doctor, but he'd

given up any idea of medical school when his high-school sweetheart, Jenny, had got pregnant. They had married and both studied to be paramedics, while looking after their newborn daughter, moving to Austin from North Carolina.

They'd had high hopes to eventually move to Alaska so that Kody could become a flying paramedic and there had been talk that perhaps one day he'd go to medical school.

All the plans had been in place, but then, when their daughter had turned two, Jenny had got sick and the doctors had found the cancer in her ovaries. It had been a short battle and all their dreams had gone.

Just like that.

It was just him and his little bug, Lucy, against the world. Although Sally came and helped as much as she could, Sally wanted to be a doctor and wouldn't be able to help with Lucy anymore. And Sally was moving on with his best friend, Ross. They were happy and he couldn't begrudge them happiness. He had been annoyed at first, when Ross had made a move and taken up with his little sister, but not overtly unhappy about it. He was just going to let Ross think that every once in a while.

Sally deserved happiness and Ross was a great guy.

Still, he was envious of them, but he couldn't let another woman into his life. He wouldn't put Lucy at risk if things didn't work out. He'd dated since Jenny died, just nothing more than a couple of dates that had gone nowhere because Lucy was his priority.

So, here he was, a widower, father and a paramedic, who really wished he could do more to help the lives he tried to save when he was first on the scene.

Dr. Fraser will save him.

And the fleeting thought of Dr. Sandra Fraser made his pulse beat a bit faster. The moment he laid eyes on Sandra something came to life. There was a spark, something electric, and he wanted to get to know her.

It was just she didn't seem interested and he couldn't introduce a woman to Lucy when there was a chance it wouldn't last. He wouldn't allow Lucy to get hurt like that.

Still, Sandra made him think about what could be.

Don't think about it.

Kody ran his hand through his hair and sighed as he turned back toward the ambulance bay. He had no time for relationships and really hadn't had the inclination since Jenny had died five years ago.

Lucy and taking care of her were his top priority.

That was all that mattered.

"You were a long time," his partner, Robbie, said. "Did boss lady tear you a new one?"

The mention of boss lady made a few of the other paramedics hanging around their rigs laugh and that made Kody a bit uneasy. If he had known it bothered her so much, he wouldn't have called her that.

He hadn't been lying when he'd said he was no stranger to being called "joke" names that apparently weren't supposed to cause harm but did.

Like half-breed or Injun. Everything that pointed out he was part-Cherokee, as if it were a shameful thing, as if it were something he shouldn't be proud of, when he was dang proud of that fact.

"Hey, cool it, Robbie," Kody said quietly.

"Cool what?" Robbie asked, confused.

"The boss lady."

Robbie shrugged. "It's just a joke."

"Yeah, well, what're we, like, twelve? And no, she didn't tear me a new one. She was so busy stabilizing our patient that she didn't release me until now."

"Sorry," Robbie said. "No offense."

Kody didn't respond and helped Robbie clean up the rig and make sure it was stocked for the next shift. Kody was glad his shift was almost over. He wanted to get home to Lucy, especially before the storm that was threatening to come in hit.

If there was any kind of disaster, he was on call to be first on the scene. He was hoping for a quiet night.

"You okay, man?" Robbie asked.

"I'm okay." Kody smiled. "Just tired."

Robbie nodded. "Well, let's get back to the station house. It was a long shift and an accident involving a car and a cow really wasn't a great ending."

Kody half smiled and nodded. "You're right."

It had been a bizarre ending to a long shift, but also a good ending since he'd got to see Dr. Fraser. Even though there was no way he'd act on anything, it was nice to see her and admire her, even from a distance.

And that was all it could ever be.

Admiration from a distance.

CHAPTER TWO

"DADDY!"

Kody was nearly barreled over when he walked in the front door of his small west-Austin home. Even though Lucy was a big girl of seven, he still scooped her up in his arms and gave her a kiss. Lucy looked more and more like his late wife, Jenny, every day. Strawberry blond hair, with curls and his blue eyes.

"You did your nails," Kody exclaimed as he checked her hand and saw the wildly garish colors on her tiny nails.

"Aunt Sally helped," Lucy said.

"It's about time," Sally, his little sister, said, coming in from the kitchen. "Ross is waiting for me. He's driving me to the station."

"Sorry, Sweet Pea. I was held up at the hospital." Kody set Lucy down. "My patient was a passenger in a head-on collision with a Texas longhorn."

Sally cocked one of her finely arched brows. "A cow?"

"Oh, no, was the cow hurt?" Lucy asked.

Kody plastered a fake smile on his face. "No. The cow's fine."

Then he shot a look to his sister and shook his head. No, the longhorn did not fare well at all. Sally made a face.

"Well, I fed Lucy…macaroni, beef and tomato sauce casserole," Sally said.

"Thanks," Kody said dryly as Lucy plopped herself on the couch to read her book.

"That doesn't sound appreciative," Sally teased.

"Sorry. It is, Sweet Pea. It was just a very long rescue. Very messy and now I get to eat a casserole of beef."

What he didn't mention was his run-in with Sandra was partly to blame. He didn't need Sally teasing him about Dr. Fraser.

It was bad enough that Ross bugged him about dating again, he didn't need Sally siding with her new boyfriend.

"Hey, I didn't know you were dealing with a cow accident at work."

"I know." Kody scrubbed his hand over his face and there was a crack of thunder in the distance, before the slow and then fast patter of rain on his metal roof.

Great.

Sally winced. "Well, I'd better get home so Ross can take me to the station. I am working another twenty-four-hour shift again."

"It's part of the job," Kody teased.

"Don't I know it." Sally walked over to Lucy and gave her a kiss on the head. "Later, love bug."

"Bye, Aunt Sally."

"Thanks, Sally." Kody walked his sister out as she dashed from his front porch to her car on the street.

Kody let out a heavy sigh and headed to the kitchen. He was going to heat up some of the dinner and then make sure that Lucy's grandparents, Jenny's parents, who had moved from North Carolina to be with Jenny and Lucy, were around so that he could drop Lucy off there if he was called in.

He was one of the few medics at the station who had advanced life-support training as a tactical paramedic and wilderness emergency medical technician.

If there was flash flooding, he'd be called in.

I should just take Lucy there now.

He knew he'd be called in. It was only a matter of time and he was thankful his in-laws were so close.

At first, he'd grumbled when Jenny's parents, Ted and Myrtle, had decided to follow him and Jenny to Austin, but he was so glad they had and that they'd stayed. They were a huge source of help to him and they'd got to be with Jenny when she'd passed.

What had started out as a strained relationship when he and Jenny had been in high school was now a close relationship. He thought of them as a second set of parents.

They'd been his rock here in Austin, before Sally had followed him out here after her divorce.

Davises are cursed in love, apparently.

He punched in the number and Myrtle answered.

"Hey, it's Kody."

"Kody! So glad to hear from you. I take it you're on call tonight?" Myrtle asked.

"I am and it's raining hard. I'm worried there's going to be some flash flooding up in hill country."

"Bring Lucy over whenever. It's been a while since she had a sleepover with Grammy and Gramps."

"Thanks, Myrtle. I'm going to have dinner and spend some time with her before I bring her over."

"See you soon, Kody."

Kody ended the call and then took the plate that Sally had made up for him. He zapped it in the microwave and then sank uneasily into the kitchen chair. There was a flash of lightning and Lucy came scurrying into the kitchen.

"Hey, love bug. Do you think you could pass me some Parmesan cheese from the fridge?"

"Sure, Daddy." Lucy opened the fridge and

handed him the Parmesan cheese, taking her seat right next to him. He smiled at her. She reminded him of Jenny so much.

"Promise me you'll open your heart again," Jenny whispered.

"Don't say that. How could I do that?" he asked.

Jenny smiled weakly. "I don't want you to be alone. I don't want Lucy to grow up without a mother."

A lump formed in his throat and he shook the memory away. He was breaking his one promise to Jenny. She'd wanted him to be happy again. She'd wanted a mother for Lucy, but he couldn't risk opening his heart again.

He couldn't risk losing another mother figure for Lucy.

He couldn't risk his heart again.

But you're lonely.

"You okay, Daddy?"

"Fine." Kody smiled, but it was a fake smile for Lucy.

He was lonely and it had been five years since Jenny died, but how could he move on from her? How could he let his heart open again to that kind of pain? That kind of grief over the possibility of losing someone else he loved?

He just couldn't.

"So, there's a bad rainstorm…"

Lucy sighed. "I know. You have to go help others. Does this mean a sleepover at Grammy's?"

Kody chuckled. "It sure does. How about you go pack an overnight bag and after I finish dinner we'll head over to Grammy's?"

"Okay." Lucy ran off to her room.

He'd lucked out on having such a great, well-adjusted kid and he credited that to Jenny's kind disposition and to all the help he'd had in raising her.

As he finished his dinner and cleaned up, his cell phone buzzed with a text message. He was being called in for emergency duty. There was some flash flooding, just as he'd expected. He flicked on the coffee machine and jammed in a pod. It was going to be a long night.

While it whirred and hummed Lucy came out of her room with her bag ready.

"I'm ready to go!" she said brightly.

Kody grinned. "Good. I'll just get my coffee in a travel mug and we'll get out of here. Go put on your rubber boots and dig out the umbrella."

"Right, Dad."

Kody stifled a yawn. Yep, tonight was going to be a long, long night.

Sandra had her wipers going at maximum speed, but she still couldn't see through the rain that was coming down in sheets.

I should've just stayed at the hospital.

The thing was, her shift was over, Mr. McIver had died and after what had happened today she was emotionally drained. For the first time in a long time she'd decided to actually go home instead of lingering at the hospital, even though she hated going home to an empty house.

You're the one who bought a ranch outside the city.

She hadn't been thinking straight when she'd bought the ranch house on an old cattle range when she'd moved out here from

San Diego. Although she'd always loved the country over the city. She'd had hopes of buying a large piece of land outside San Diego where her kids could grow and run.

And her heart hurt when she thought about that.

Kids.

She desperately wanted them, but, after rounds and rounds of IVF treatments that hadn't worked and too many miscarriages that had broken her heart, she knew that she would never have kids. She wanted to adopt, as she was adopted, but it was about the time she'd started the process of adoption her now ex-husband had suddenly announced that he didn't want kids. And she'd realized Alex never had been the right man for her.

She wanted kids and he didn't, at least not ones that weren't biologically his.

And that was the reason he'd said he wanted a divorce: because he couldn't open his heart to someone else's child. He wanted his own and she couldn't give him that.

She'd had to walk away, though it had broken her heart to do so. It had been the right thing to do.

Alex had made her feel, for an inkling of a second, that she had somehow failed as a woman. It had taken her a year to shake that thought of failure from her mind. Staying in San Diego and working with him had never let her truly heal. Which was why she'd bought this old ranch outside Austin and moved away from San Diego.

There was no family keeping her in San Diego anymore. Her beloved adoptive parents were gone. It was just her and she had to do something for herself. So she'd decided to go to the place of her birth. To find roots, and what better place to find roots than a beautiful piece of land on the outskirts of the city?

Of course, now, with this crazy rain, she was really regretting her choice of living outside the city.

Sandra leaned over her steering wheel, trying to peer through the sheets of rain. Thankfully it wasn't completely dark out, but the sun was setting behind the gray rain clouds. She had to get home soon, before it got dark and made it completely impossible to see anything.

She slowed down as she approached a small one-lane bridge and pulled over as a driver coming in the opposite direction crossed over.

There was a crack of thunder and a rumbling sound, which made Sandra's blood run cold. She glanced out of her driver's-side window in time to see a wave of mud washing down over the hill.

Oh, my God.

And there was nothing she could do. She just closed her eyes as the mud hit her car, tipping it over and over down the embankment toward the small creek that was swollen and overflowing with water.

Her life, her lonely life, flashed before her eyes and she knew right then and there she was going to die.

"Jesus!" Kody climbed out of his car. He had just passed that car while it waited for him to cross the bridge when he heard the rumbling behind him. He looked in his rearview mirror to see the mud from the side of the hill come washing down over the small SUV.

He instantly called into the dispatch for help.

"I'm on Tarry Cross Road West and there's a car that's been washed down into Burl's Creek."

"Gotcha, Kody. We'll be there as soon as we can. Some of the roads out that way have been washed out."

"Roger, I'll see what I can do to help." Kody ended the call and popped open his trunk, grabbing a tool he kept for smashing open windows. He made his way carefully over to the mudflow that had stopped, for now, but he knew any moment it could give way again.

The rain was dissipating, and the SUV was on its side, but not far down the embankment. It wouldn't have taken much for it to become dislodged and be swallowed up by the creek. He made his way to the driver's-side door and peered inside. There was a lone passenger, unconscious, who was buckled in and on her side.

Kody tapped on the window. "Hey! You okay?"

She roused and looked toward him. His blood ran cold when he saw who was trapped in the SUV.

"Sandra!" he shouted. "Are you okay?"

She nodded but motioned she was stuck.

"Cover your face," he said and held up his tool that was used to break windows.

Sandra nodded her understanding and grabbed her jacket, shielding her face and arms. Once Kody was sure that she was safe he smashed open the window. It was an older vehicle, so the window broke easily. He cleaned away all the jagged remnants.

"You okay?" he asked.

"No, my head," she murmured. "And I seem to be stuck in my seat belt."

Kody handed her a knife. "I can't climb in there—if I do it might dislodge the vehicle and it and you will tumble down into the water."

She nodded and took the knife, sawing away at her seat belt; sliding a bit, she held her own and grabbed her purse, snaking it around her body.

"Take my hand," Kody said.

Sandra reached up and he carefully helped her out of her SUV and into his arms. He held her close and backed away from the SUV and out of the mud. Just as they got back onto the pavement, there was a crack and her SUV continued its tumble down the embankment.

She buried her head in his neck and let out a whimper as he held her close.

"It's okay. I got you." His heart was hammering, and he was trying to catch his breath. All he could do was stand there and hold her. It was comforting to hold her, and he didn't want to even think about what would've happened had he not been here.

"We should get out of here," Sandra murmured, but still holding on to his jacket, her body still curled up tight against his chest.

"You're right."

"I live just on the other side of the bridge. Down Denham Road." Her voice shook as she spoke, and he didn't blame her.

"The bridge is washed out, but I know another way." He carried her to his car and helped her get settled into the back. He opened his trunk and tossed his tools back in there, before grabbing a blanket.

He climbed into the driver's seat and handed her the blanket. She was wadding up some tissues for what looked like a superficial head wound.

"Thanks," she said, her voice trembling.

"You're safe. Let's get you to your house and then I can call the team and tell them you're safe and I'll make sure that's just a superficial wound."

"Thanks." She held the tissues against her forehead.

"Sorry about your vehicle," he said.

"It's just my SUV that's totaled," she muttered. "That's a small price to pay for my life."

Kody nodded, but his pulse was still racing. He couldn't believe she'd been so close to death like that, and the thought of her losing her life terrified him and he didn't know why.

Probably because you know her and you watched it happen.

Kody pulled away from the scene of the mudslide and took his time making his way carefully down the road and turning down the other road that led to Denham, but the moment he turned the corner, it was gone. The road was washed away and Burl's Creek now looked like an angry river gurgling and rushing past them.

"Well, I guess we can…" There was a rumble and Kody watched in horror as the road behind them washed out. They were trapped on a small stretch of road and Burl's Creek was inching toward them.

"We have to go on foot. There's a small cabin not far from here. It's on the edge of my property. It's high ground," she said.

Kody nodded. Sandra helped him grab what he needed from his truck, but it was hard for her since one hand was holding the now-wet blob of tissues against her head wound.

"Just lead the way, Sandra. I'll follow," he ordered.

Sandra nodded and headed up a trail off the road, higher than the river, up onto the range. It was a slippery climb, but she seemed to know her way up the stony embankment, through the cottonwood trees, and eventually they were out on the plains. It looked as if it was an old cattle ranch.

"My house is in that direction, but we'd have to cross the water to get to it," Sandra shouted.

Kody nodded, but he couldn't make it out, not through the rain, which was getting heavier. However, she had led them right—there was a cabin about five hundred feet away and they should be safe there, provided he could get a fire started and figure out a way to contact help.

"Let's go." He slung his pack of supplies over his shoulder and without thinking he took her hand and led her through the wind and rain to the cabin. She pulled out her ring of keys and unlocked the door.

Kody followed her in.

The cabin was dark, but it was dry, and it was shelter.

"There's no electricity yet," she explained through chattering teeth. "I was planning on having it renovated soon, to rent it out."

"It has a fireplace, so I can get to building us a fire." He set down his bag and Sandra sat on a sheet-covered chair, pulling the damp blanket around her tighter.

He pulled out his fire starters and was relieved that there was a bit of wood still in the cabin, so it would be dry. He knelt down and built a pyramid and set his homemade fire starters under. It didn't take long before they had a fire going.

He pulled off his jacket and set it on the floor, while he rummaged in his bag for some rope. Something they could hang their wet clothes on so the fire could dry them. He pulled out the twine and set about making a makeshift clothesline.

"You've thought of everything," Sandra said. She was visibly shivering, and the tissue was blood-soaked and wet under her fingers.

"Come closer to the fire and I'll check out that wound."

"It's superficial," she said.

"Dr. Fraser, get over here. Now." He shook his head and she came closer to the fire and sat on the floor in front of him.

"I've never heard you be so forceful before," she said and there was a twinkle in her eye, like one he'd never seen, and she was smiling. He liked her smile.

"I think you have a concussion," he said dryly.

"Why do you say that?"

"You're joking with me." He smiled at her and she laughed softly.

"I don't think it's a concussion. I think the adrenaline is wearing off."

"So you're saying it's nerves?" he asked.

"I don't know." She laughed. "Thank you for saving my life."

"It's my job."

"Still, if you hadn't been there..." She trailed off and he knew what she was thinking because he thought it too. She would've died.

"Hold still," he said as he gently peeled away the wet tissue to examine the wound. She was right, it was superficial, and it had mostly stopped bleeding.

"Superficial, isn't it?" she asked.

"Doctors make the worst patients," he muttered as he pulled out some antibiotic ointment and gauze.

She laughed again. "I suppose we do."

Kody didn't respond and bandaged up her head. "There, you're all done."

"Thanks," she said and pulled the blanket tighter. "The fire feels good. You have a lot of stuff in that bag of tricks."

"I have wilderness survival skills training and am a tactical paramedic."

"Wow," she said, sounding impressed. "I usually don't meet a lot of paramedics with that level of training in an urban setting."

"Well, when I got my certifications, I was preparing for a different life than being an urban EMT. Of course, fate sometimes has a way of kicking you in your soft spot." He snapped the lid shut on his first-aid kit.

"I hear you," she said. "I never thought in a million years that I would be here, in Austin, and living on an old cattle ranch."

"Where did you expect to be?" he asked.

She cocked an eyebrow. "If I tell you, then you have to tell me about this different so-called life you were preparing for. Tit for tat."

"Tit for tat?" he asked.

"Yeah, I'm not going to give you my life story without something in return. Just know that it stays between us."

"Deal," he said, because they had to kill time somehow and the rain was starting up again something fierce. At least he knew that Lucy was safe, so he didn't have to worry about that. And he wouldn't mind getting to know Dr. Fraser better. He admired her and she was a closed book. "So, where did you expect to be? How has your life gone sideways?"

"I got divorced," she said. "And we worked together in San Diego and I couldn't stand seeing him all the time, so I came here."

"There's more to it than that."

"What do you mean?" she asked carefully.

"San Diego is a large city. You transfer to another hospital—you don't pick up everything and move a couple of states away."

Sandra sighed. "Fine. I couldn't have kids… He didn't want to adopt. It was a hard and emotional breakup and I knew to put it properly behind me I'd have to leave."

"So why Austin?"

"I was adopted and grew up with my parents in San Diego, but I was born here. Since my adoptive parents are gone, I thought I would come home. Besides, a few months ago my ex remarried and is having the biological family he always wanted."

"And you desperately wanted kids," he said softly.

She nodded and he could see the tears in her eyes. "I did, but it wasn't meant to be. I can't get pregnant. Trust me, we tried, and I went through a lot of procedures. He found someone else who gave him the kids I couldn't."

"Now I get it."

"You get what?" she asked.

"Why you moved from San Diego and why you bought an old cattle ranch in the middle of nowhere." He reached into his bag and dug out a couple of granola bars. He tossed her one.

"You get that?" she teased, opening her granola bar and taking a bite.

"I think so, and I see the appeal. Living in a city is not at all how I planned my life." He leaned back against the wall. "I wanted to be an air paramedic in Alaska."

She raised her eyebrows. "Wow, that sounds adventurous and explains the wilderness training."

"It was going to be." He smiled. "Of course, then my high-school girlfriend got pregnant when we were twenty-one, so we got married and both became paramedics. There wasn't much work in North Carolina and with a baby we couldn't pursue our dreams of Alaska right away. I took a job in Austin…" He trailed off because it was hard even now to talk about Jenny. It brought back all those memories. All their hopes and dreams that never saw fruition.

He never talked about this with anyone. Ever. Those were his hopes and dreams. Their hopes and dreams, Jenny's and his.

He never shared Jenny with anyone but her parents, Sally, and Lucy; Jenny and their plans he kept locked away. It was easier to cope with the grief that way.

Is it?

"What happened?" Sandra asked softly.

"My wife died of cancer five years ago." And he fought back the tears that were threatening to fall. Even after all this time, admitting it was hard.

"I'm so sorry."

Kody nodded. "At least I have my daughter, Lucy. I have a piece of my wife still."

"So, Alaska is on hold?"

He nodded. "My late wife's parents followed us from North Carolina to Austin and are a huge help to me with Lucy. I could never take Lucy away from them."

"I never knew you had a child."

"You never asked."

"No. I suppose I didn't, but I haven't made a lot of friends here in Austin," she admitted.

"You will."

A strange looked passed briefly over her face. "We'll see."

"Well, I'm your friend."

"Are you?" she asked.

"Of course. I don't talk about my personal life with just anyone."

What he didn't say was that he didn't share any of this with anyone. He wasn't even sure why he was telling Sandra all of this. Maybe because she'd let down her guard too and it felt good to let it all out. He'd been bottling it up for so long.

"Well, there are flying paramedics in Texas. Perhaps you can get your license?"

Kody scrubbed a hand over his face. "It's costly and you need to invest a lot of time in learning to fly. Perhaps one day. Right now, Lucy needs me."

"You're a good dad." She smiled at him, her brown eyes twinkling in the flickering firelight. "I misjudged you."

"How?" he asked.

"You were this fun-loving, charismatic guy. Men I know like that often play the field."

He was shocked. "I've never been a player. There's only been Jenny, and a handful of dates I went on about a year ago that went nowhere. That's hardly playboy material."

"I understand that now," she said. "And I'm glad you're not. Guys like that aren't good for the heart." She blushed. "What I mean is…"

He chuckled. "I understand. Still, it does

secretly please me you thought I was charming enough to be a player."

And it did. It made his pulse quicken in an-
ticipation that she thought he was something
of a bad boy. That she thought of him like
that. That she thought about him more than
just as a paramedic who annoyed her.

Sandra smiled at him; there was a dimple
in her cheek and her chocolate-brown eyes lit
with a sparkle he'd never seen. It made him
feel warm; it shook away the remnants of the
pain that were threatening to take over. The
grief that he'd learned to compartmentalize in
the last five years since Jenny slipped away.

"You have a beautiful smile, Sandra. Really beautiful," he whispered.

"Thanks."

"You should smile more."

"Why? Because I'm only pretty when I
smile?"

"No! No, you're beautiful all the time. I've
always thought so. I just like it when you
smile at me."

And before he knew what he was doing
he reached out to touch her face. She let out

a little sigh and she leaned forward, kissing him and sending an electric buzz through him that he hadn't felt in a long, long time.

Sandra didn't mean to kiss Kody. When he'd told her she was beautiful and touched her, she'd lost all control. Kissing him had never been in the plans.

Liar. It so was.

She'd thought about it once or twice or more since she'd met him. She'd just never thought she'd act on it.

Liar. You so did.

"I'm sorry," she said, quickly breaking off the kiss. And she was. She didn't know what had come over her. She was so moved by his story. So moved by the emotion he stirred in her, she couldn't hold back. It had been so long since she'd felt this way about anyone.

She'd thought, after Alex and her failed marriage, that she would never feel that way about another man again. She was so burned out, so lonely, but then Kody had shared a piece of himself with her. She'd shared her vulnerability and he in turn had shared his own.

It meant a lot.

"Don't be sorry," Kody said and then he cupped her face in his hands and kissed her back. She rose to her knees and he rose to meet her. Their bodies pressed together. His kiss was tender at first, but then urgent.

And she responded in kind to that urgency.

That need that she had been trying so hard to ignore. She hoped that if they just shared this moment of release, she could move on. He'd be the first man she slept with since Alex, and Kody was the exact type of man to help her move past the pain that held her back. Still, the thought that Kody was the first since Alex scared her. Being intimate and vulnerable was overwhelming, but she wanted—needed—this moment. She wanted to move on, and she was glad that it was with Kody. She moved her hands down his back, slipping them under his shirt.

"Sandra, are you sure?" His voice was husky.

"I'm sure. I know that you can't promise

me anything and I can't do that either, but I think we both need this."

Kody didn't respond vocally, but kissed her again, making her blood sing with need. His hands were in her hair and then on her back as he pressed her down against the blanket on the floor, in front of the fire.

The only sounds were crackling fire, the roaring rain and her pulse thundering in her ears as her body came alive under his touch. Sandra melted against his kisses and there was a frenzied need to be just skin to skin with him.

To have no layers between them.

Just warmth and touch.

Human contact.

A groan slipped past Kody's lips as her hands slid inside the waistband of his jeans. She undid the button and the fly and then he pulled off her sweater. It was a joint effort. No words were needed. They both knew what they wanted.

The only sounds between them were their hungry kisses.

She knew what she wanted in this moment.

And that was Kody.

She wanted to feel every inch of him. Feel him buried deep inside her. His kisses left her lips, burning a path of flames down her neck, over her collarbone to her breasts. She arched her back. She was ready, so ready for this to happen. So ready for him to claim her and that it was Kody for this first time since Alex. Since her heart was broken.

She wrapped her legs around his waist, letting him silently know she burned for him, just as she knew he burned for her.

"Are you sure, Sandra?" he asked again.

"Yes." She kissed him, running her hands through his silky black hair. "So sure."

Kody didn't kiss her, just held her locked in his gaze. She was lost deep in his eyes as he entered her. Sandra cried out, but not from pain, from the release she felt at trusting someone to be intimate with her again. The sense of vulnerability he made her feel.

As if she didn't have to hold back in this moment. It was freeing. It was hot and frenzied and exactly what she needed. For far too long she'd been holding back, trying to find the bits and pieces that Alex had stolen from her when he'd cheated on her, when he'd told her that she was a disappointment for not being able to carry a child.

Kody didn't expect any of that from her and it was freeing. So freeing it was heady. The feel of his strong hands on her body, on her hips, guiding her in a rhythm they both found pleasurable. She held on to his shoulders, not wanting to let him go, not wanting this moment to end.

It didn't take long, and she climaxed around him, crying out, and he joined her soon after. He rested his head on her shoulder for a moment, before rolling over on his back, trying to catch his breath, his arm wrapped around her shoulder.

"We should probably get dressed again, so we don't freeze to death," she said. Not that she wanted to get up. Her legs felt like jelly and her head was spinning. She pulled on her clothes and then grabbed the blanket.

Kody tended the fire and threw on some more wood. He'd put on his jeans, but not his shirt. She arched an eyebrow in question.

"It's better for body heat." He smiled and kissed her forehead. "Thank you."

Heat bloomed in her cheeks. "Thank you too. I hope… I hope this won't be awkward at work. This can only be a one-time thing."

"I know and, no, it won't be awkward." He smiled and wrapped his arm around her. They lay back down on the hard floor. He let her use his shirt as a pillow, as her head was throbbing still, and he tucked the blanket around them. He spooned her from behind.

"That feels nice," she murmured.

"Good," he said gently. "Try to rest. Hopefully someone will find us in the morning. If not, we should be able to walk to your place and let people know we're still alive."

"What about your little girl?" Sandra asked.

"She's with her grandma and grandpa. She's safe."

"Good."

No more words were needed, and Sandra slipped into a peaceful sleep as she hadn't had in a long, long time.

CHAPTER THREE

"KODY!"

Kody woke to someone screaming his name.

"Kody!"

He blinked as sunlight streamed in through the open window. It was blinding and right in his eye.

Where the heck am I?

And it took him a moment to realize that it was morning and that Dr. Sandra Foster was curled up beside him. It all came flooding back to him then. He'd made love to Sandra. He'd become lost in the moment after they'd opened up and shared and he'd completely lost his head and all sense of reason.

Completely.

He'd never opened up about Jenny before and he'd never thought he could ever be with someone again, but Sandra had got through to him.

It had been a long time since he'd wanted someone, but reaching through to Sandra and understanding why she held people at a distance just made him admire her drive and determination more.

And she looked so peaceful, sleeping beside him. A touch of pink in her cheeks, her lips parted as she breathed softly.

He remembered the touch of those lips against his and the warmth of her embrace. The feel of her nails in his back.

He wanted her again.

You can't have her again. One time only, remember?

And he had to keep reminding himself of that. This was a one-time thing. A moment of comfort between the two of them.

That was all it could be.

And he'd thought one time would be enough. It scared him that he wanted her so fiercely again.

"Kody!"

He recognized that voice. It was Sally calling him. He got up, trying not to disturb Sandra, and his back protested after having spent the night on a hardwood floor. He went to the door and walked outside. The temperature had dropped, breaking the heat wave that had been plaguing Austin the last couple of days. The breeze was cool and earthy, but also there was not a cloud in the sky, which meant the risk of flash flooding was past them.

He saw a team of first responders and a fire truck down the hill. And part of the first responders was his sister, Sally, who was calling his name frantically.

"Sweet Pea! Here!" He waved and Sally came running up the hill. She ran straight into his arms.

"Oh, thank God!" she said. "When I saw your truck… I was worried you were washed away, like the other one farther down the creek."

"The SUV?"

Sally nodded, stepping back. "Yeah, we couldn't find a body, though. Ross has his team looking farther downstream of Burl's Creek."

"That's Dr. Fraser's SUV. She was hit by a mudslide and I got her out." Kody turned and saw that Sandra was standing in the door, looking just as confused as he first was when he'd woken up this morning.

"What's going on?" Sandra asked.

"We're being rescued," he said over his shoulder before turning back to Sally. "You can call off Ross's search party. Dr. Fraser is fine."

"Is she hurt?" Sally asked, noticing his crude bandage job on Sandra.

"She was hurt, but it was superficial."

"Still, it should be looked at. Both of you need to be checked out. If you have any cuts, you'll need a course of antibiotics. You know mudslides contain bacteria that can contain flesh-eating properties," Sally stated.

"Right," Kody said, exhausted. He ran his hand through his hair and winced.

"You okay?" Sally asked, worried.

"Just stiff. Please take care of Dr. Fraser."

Sally nodded and approached Sandra. He

could hear them talking—Sandra was a bit standoffish. More like her old self, but he couldn't shake the image of how it had been last night. When it had been just the two of them, as one.

His blood heated as he thought about her in his arms. The way her lips had felt on his and how tender she'd been.

It had been a long time since he'd been with anyone.

There hadn't been anyone since Jenny, and in a way he felt guilty. Even though Jenny had told him to move on, to find happiness after she died, there was a part of him that still felt guilty. As if he had cheated on her memory.

You didn't. Jenny's been gone for five years.

And it was a one-time thing. He had to keep reminding himself of that. It was a one-time thing. Only he was fooling himself. Why did he ever think that once would be enough?

Either way, it had to be.

He'd promised Sandra that.

Sally helped Sandra out of the cabin.

"Let's just go to the hospital to get checked out, Dr. Fraser," Sally said gently.

Sandra nodded and briefly glanced at him.

"I'll come too," Kody assured her. "We both should be checked out."

Sandra didn't say much. It was almost as if she was angry with him. He had promised that there would be no awkwardness between them, but that seemed to be the opposite of what was happening here.

And he didn't like it one bit.

They were taken to the hospital where Sandra worked. She was immediately taken off to have a CT scan; even if she was constantly insisting to the trauma doctors on duty that the wound was superficial, they wouldn't listen to her. It was protocol, and she had some symptoms of a concussion.

Kody was checked over and Sally went off to tell his in-laws and Lucy that he was okay and had been found. They were eventually placed side by side in the same trauma pod, just a curtain separating them.

He snuck out of his bed and opened the

curtain next to him. Sandra was lying in bed and waiting for test results. She looked highly annoyed. Those delicious lips of hers were pursed and she was staring up at the ceiling, her hands folded across her stomach.

"Hey," he said gently.

She glanced at him. "I told them it was nothing, but they won't listen to me."

He chuckled. "I told you that doctors are the worst patients."

She smiled quickly then, before it disappeared. "Are you okay?"

"They ran a blood test to see. I had a scrape on my leg. I didn't even feel it, but it was dirty…wading around in the mud trying to save people's lives." He winked at her. "I'll probably get some antibiotics via IV."

She nodded and held up her hand that had an IV started. "Probably, like me. Just waiting until they tell me the CT was clear and I can get a cab to take me home since my car was washed down Burl's Creek."

"They found it and are retrieving it. Your insurance should cover it."

Sandra sighed. "So that female paramedic, is she your partner?"

"Sally? No, I don't work with her."

Sandra frowned. "She seemed so worried about you. More than a colleague should be..."

He grinned then. "Dr. Fraser, are you jealous of my baby sister?"

Her eyes widened. "Your sister? You called her Sweet Pea!"

"It's a name my entire family calls her." He chuckled. "She's my sister, which is why we're not partners and why we never work on the same shift. She moved out here after her divorce and she helps with my daughter as well. Also, she's stolen my best friend, Ross, out from under me too."

"Oh." He thought that he saw a brief moment of relief there.

"You were jealous, weren't you?" he teased.

She glared at him indignantly. "I was not. Okay, perhaps just a bit. I was worried that I..."

"What?" he asked.

She lowered her voice. "That I slept with

someone else's partner. I never want to be the other woman."

"No need to worry," he said gently.

That struck a chord with him. He couldn't blame her for feeling guilty. Heck, he felt guilty for what had happened, and he was a widower, but there was a part of him, deep down, that thought she sort of was another woman compared to Jenny. He had never felt this way about someone since Jenny died. It scared him that she'd got under his skin.

"You okay?" she asked, now looking concerned. "Are you seeing someone? We never discussed that last night…"

He shook his head and fluffed it off. "No. I'm not. I don't have time for a relationship. I have my daughter to think of."

Which was true. He did. There was no time to date and he didn't want to bring someone into his daughter's life, someone who might be taken away again. It was bad enough putting his own heart at risk, but also putting his daughter at risk?

"I don't have time either," Sandra said. "I

meant it when I said no promises. It was one night, but that's all."

He nodded, but still wasn't sure how to process all the emotions he was feeling in this moment.

"Well, I should get back to my bed. Sally said that my in-laws are bringing my daughter in to see me."

Sandra smiled. "Thank you again, Kody."

"For what?"

"For saving my life. I appreciate it."

He didn't know how to respond to that. "Get some rest and I'll see you around."

Kody stepped back and closed the curtain dividing their beds, but not all the way—he could still see her through a small crack. He had saved her life and wanted to keep an eye on her. Truth be told, he liked being able to see her. He would see her around, but he was going to make sure that he went out of his way not to interact with her too much. Yeah, he'd promised her things wouldn't be awkward between them and it was a promise he wasn't sure that he could keep.

Not when the guilt of sleeping with someone who was not Jenny was eating away at him.

Sandra dozed off as she waited for the results of her CT. The antibiotics were also making her tired, plus spending a night on a hardwood floor wasn't exactly a comfortable experience.

Being with Kody was a comfortable experience, though.

It had been more than comfortable. It had been the best she'd ever had. What she'd had with her ex-husband was nothing compared to what she'd enjoyed with Kody in the cabin.

Her blood heated just thinking about his hands on her, his kisses and the way he'd made her feel as if she mattered.

She wanted more than just one night.

And she tried not to think about that.

She wasn't going to get involved with anyone again. There was nothing she could offer them. One day, she'd get some money saved and she'd pursue adoption, even if adopting as a single woman was difficult.

She didn't care. She was going to try.

She'd been adopted as a baby and had the best parents, both of whom were gone. She was pretty much alone in this world.

Sandra glanced over at Kody. She could see him lying in his hospital bed through the crack in the curtains; he'd been given some IV antibiotics and looked as if he was drifting in and out of sleep. A warm feeling swirled around in the pit of her stomach.

She wished she could trust him. She wished she could open her heart again, but she wasn't sure that he was ready for that either. She'd had no idea that he was a widower. It had changed her whole perspective about him. For the better. She'd been wrong about him.

He's off-limits.

Kody had a daughter and wasn't interested in dating. He probably wasn't lonely like her. He had a family who cared about him.

Sandra had no one.

It was better this way.

"Dr. Fraser?" Dr. Coombs whispered as she came through the drapes. "How are you feeling?"

"I'm good."

Dr. Coombs checked her IV. "You're almost done, and your CT is clean, but the chief of surgery wants you to take a couple of days off, just to get some rest from your ordeal."

"It wasn't an ordeal," Sandra stated.

"I know, but it's doctor's orders." Dr. Coombs smiled, but Sandra could tell she was nervous.

And she couldn't help but think of what Kody had said to her about how doctors were the worst patients. He was so right, and she smiled to herself. Too bad nothing could happen between them.

"Fine." Sandra sighed. "So I can go?"

Dr. Coombs nodded. "I'll take out your IV and you're free to go."

"Thank you, Megan."

Dr. Coombs's eyes widened in surprise. "You're welcome, Dr. Fraser."

It was true Sandra tried to keep everyone at a distance to protect herself from being hurt, from losing people, but maybe if she was a bit more friendly with the staff she wouldn't feel so alone.

Sandra lay back while Dr. Coombs took out

her IV. She glanced over at Kody's bed and then saw an elderly couple with a young girl come in. They stopped at the charge desk and then the little girl squealed, and Kody sat up as the little girl with strawberry blond hair ran and climbed up into his bed, throwing her arms around him.

"Daddy! I was so worried."

It warmed her heart and filled her with a sense of longing as she watched Kody reunite with his daughter and his late wife's parents, who seemed just as emotional and glad for his safety. They were a family.

Just like when she'd seen Kody with his sister.

And Sandra envied him that family. She was jealous and it made her miss her parents so much.

"You're all done, Dr. Fraser," Dr. Coombs said.

Sandra smiled and blinked a few times, hoping that the tears that were threatening to spill didn't. The last thing she needed was for her residents to see her cry.

"Thank you, Dr. Coombs. I'll see you in

a couple of days." She took her discharge papers from Megan and grabbed her purse, which was on the table next to her bed.

She glanced one more time at Kody and his little family but couldn't see him. His mother-in-law was standing between them, almost as if his late wife were warning her to keep away.

And she would. She walked out of the ER and headed straight for the exit. There were a couple of cabs lingering and she hailed one, climbing in and giving the address, hoping that the roads were clear for her to get home.

All she wanted to do was go home and sleep. She wanted to forget what had happened last night, in the rainstorm. She wanted to forget how good it felt to be intimate with Kody, how safe she'd felt in his arms and how she wanted more.

She just couldn't have that.

She couldn't risk her heart again and she wouldn't tear apart that little girl's family.

Not for anything.

CHAPTER FOUR

Two months later

"DR. COOMBS, COULD YOU…?"

Sandra felt as if her stomach were doing countless flip-flops. She'd come down with this stomach flu and no matter what she did she couldn't shake it. And she couldn't take any more time off work. She'd taken a week off already and had thought she was feeling better, since she was usually sicker in the morning. She'd thought because of that she could handle a night shift.

Obviously she'd been wrong, because her first patient of the night smelled like a combination of hot garbage and cannabis and she found it was completely overwhelming and made her stomach turn.

"What can I do for you, Dr. Fraser?" Dr. Coombs asked.

"Could you draw blood for the patient in trauma pod two for me? He smells a bit... ripe."

Which was a polite way of saying that this particular patient's smell completely put her off. Megan had been kind to her since she'd got this stomach bug. She was always helping her out more than she should, and Sandra appreciated it.

"Dr. Fraser, are you okay?" Megan asked, worried. "You haven't been yourself the last couple of weeks."

"I'm fine." Which was a lie. She was anything but.

"I think you need to get a drink of water. You look positively green."

"It's a stomach bug, Megan... I'm fine. I thought I would be better tonight but...yeah, I'm not better. At least I'm not contagious." There was no fever and no other symptoms except the lingering queasiness. "You're right. I'll take a drink and take a sit down. I'll be fine in a moment."

Megan smiled, but looked unconvinced.

Sandra leaned against the charge desk. She had to pull herself together.

"Dr. Fraser." The nurse behind the charge desk who answered the calls from incoming ambulances looked up. "There's an ambulance on its way in with a suspected appendectomy."

"Okay. I'll meet it." She could handle a simple appendectomy. Not that an appendectomy was simple, but the operating room was cool and clean and the smell of cautery didn't make her sick to her stomach.

Yet.

"How many minutes out?"

"Five," the nurse said.

"Great." So much for trying to rest. She took a deep breath and made sure her stomach stopped churning before she quickly walked to the ambulance bay, hung up her lab coat and grabbed a yellow trauma gown, slipping it over her scrubs. She pulled on her gloves and headed outside to wait for the ambulance.

The cool night air was refreshing and not so stifling as inside the emergency department. She closed her eyes and reveled in the silence of night, not that a city like Austin really slept at all. The tall buildings were still illuminated, and she could see the state capitol lit up. It was beautiful. This was the city of her birth and she did love it here. She'd been here now six months and she didn't miss San Diego one bit.

She loved San Diego and the ocean, it was where she'd grown up, but Austin had something else and she really was beginning to feel as if she belonged here.

She took a deep breath and felt a bit nervous suddenly. She was hoping that it wasn't Kody. She hadn't seen him in two months. She hadn't seen him since they were in the hospital after the flood when she'd seen him with his family. They had promised each other after their night together that things wouldn't be awkward, but they were.

For her anyway, because thinking about seeing him made her feel anxious.

And she hadn't been able to stop thinking about him. Ever since she'd seen him with his daughter, she was longing for that kind of connection. That kind of love.

A family.

Focus.

She could hear the sirens wailing and she steeled herself for the arrival of the patient. The ambulance came down the ramp toward the ER and pulled up in front of her. The doors opened and her heart skipped a beat when Kody's back came into view. Her stomach did another flip and she took another deep breath, hoping she didn't throw up.

Anxiety and a queasy stomach didn't pair well together.

"Male, thirty, complaining of stomach pain of McBurney's point. Fever of a hundred and two, vomiting and unable to pass gas..." He trailed off as he saw her.

"Thank you." Sandra hoped that the heat she felt in her cheeks wasn't turning into a full-on blush. She didn't want this to be awkward, even though she knew that it was going to be. She'd been dreading this moment.

"I feel awful," the patient groaned.

"Does it hurt here?" Sandra asked, examining the telltale sign of an appendix about to rupture. The man screamed in pain when she released.

"Yes!" The patient groaned. "It's awful."

"Okay, we're going to get you in and do an exam." Sandra began to push the gurney.

Kody helped her wheel the patient into a trauma pod. Another one of her residents came to assist.

"Dr. McKay, set up a line with the standard protocol of antibiotics and prep an OR for an emergency appendectomy." She went to grab the ultrasound machine that they kept in the trauma room, but the motion of wheeling the ultrasound over made her head spin.

Dammit. Not now.

At least her stomach seemed a bit more settled, but she wasn't impressed with this vertigo.

"Dr. Fraser, are you okay?" Kody asked, his hand steadying her causing a trail of goose bumps to spread across her skin.

"Fine," she said quickly and moved out of his grasp. Only that was a lie. She was far from fine. The room was spinning, and it was all she could do to keep her vertigo in check. "You're released, Mr. Davis, we got it from here."

Kody nodded and stepped out of the trauma pod. At least she'd had the sense to release him this time, unlike the last time they had shared a trauma pod with a patient he'd brought in. And look how that had turned out.

Focus.

"Mr. Smythe?" Sandra said, glancing at the man's file to get his name. "The gel for the ultrasound might be cold, but I have to check."

Mr. Smythe just groaned and nodded.

Sandra squeezed the jelly onto his lower right abdomen and moved the wand carefully over McBurney's point. She could see a very swollen appendix. She snapped off the machine.

"Mr. Smythe, we're going to have to take you for surgery. Can my staff call anyone?"

"My wife...her contact is in my phone in my jacket."

A nurse grabbed his jacket and took the information down.

"We'll get you to the operating room shortly." Sandra checked his pupils. "Dr. McKay, please prep the patient for surgery. I'll meet you up there shortly."

"Yes, Dr. Fraser." Dr. McKay went to work.

The room began to spin and she knew she had to get out of there. She turned around and saw that Kody was lingering in the hall.

Why was he still here?

Mr. Smythe began to throw up and the smell hit her, making her reel, and before she knew what was happening or before she could reach Kody, the room tilted violently and her knees gave out from under her, the world around her going black before she hit the floor.

Kody was glad to see her.

He wanted to talk to her again and explain that he wasn't trying to avoid her, it was just a shift change that he had been due to do. He had been pleasantly surprised to see her on the night shift, even if she looked a little worse for wear.

She was pale and looked as if she was sick.

She'd dismissed him from the trauma pod, but his shift was over, and his partner was in no rush to leave as he was dating a nurse here, so he thought it was the perfect moment to loiter and see if he could talk to her. To tell her where he'd been and that he wasn't avoiding her.

Then she collapsed.

It happened so fast, he saw her knees give out from under her and it was all he could do to dash in there and catch her before she hit her head.

"Sandra?" He touched her face. "Sandra, speak to me."

Her eyes were fluttering, but she wasn't stirring.

"Get me a stretcher," he called out to a couple of passing orderlies. "And get an attending here—Dr. Fraser has collapsed."

The orderlies ran off and a nurse called another doctor.

"Dr. McKay, you can handle the patient, yeah?" Kody asked.

Dr. McKay nodded. "Of course. Take care

of Dr. Fraser and I'll page the on-call general surgeon."

The orderlies came with a stretcher and Kody scooped Sandra up and laid her down on the stretcher. Her blood pressure was a little slow and her skin was clammy. If she was this sick, she shouldn't be working. Why were doctors so stubborn?

Dr. Murdoch came rushing down the hall. "Kody, do you know what happened?"

"She collapsed. She seemed to have a touch of vertigo when she was examining the patient, but as she was leaving she just collapsed." Kody had noticed the way she'd moved slowly. She'd closed her eyes and tried to brace herself. That was definitely vertigo.

Dr. Coombs came out of an adjacent trauma pod. Dr. Coombs had been a nurse five years ago and had been Jenny's palliative care nurse and friend.

Megan smiled when she saw him. "Kody, I didn't know you were on night-shift duty again."

"Every so often I have to."

Megan noticed Dr. Fraser. "What happened?"

"I don't know. She fainted," he said.

"She's been feeling ill all night. She's been throwing up, but I don't think it's a virus. She's been feeling this way for a couple of weeks."

"Obviously she's not over it."

Dr. Murdoch listened to her heart as Sandra came to.

"What happened?" she asked groggily and then her eyes widened when she saw him, Dr. Murdoch and Dr. Coombs hovering over her. "Where's my patient?"

"You fainted. Dr. McKay has your appendectomy and is calling in the on-call general surgeon," Dr. Murdoch stated.

She tried to sit up, but Kody made her lie back down.

"You fainted," he said gently.

"What?" she asked.

"Dr. Fraser, is there any chance you could be pregnant?" Dr. Murdoch asked.

Kody's blood froze and all the memories of Jenny and her awful morning sickness came rushing back. The vertigo, the fainting, and Megan had said Sandra had been sick the last couple of weeks.

"No," Sandra said, laughing. "No. Not a chance."

Dr. Murdoch cocked his thick gray brows. "Nonetheless, I think we're going to run a blood panel and check for HCG levels. Until then, you're not working. I want you resting. Dr. Coombs, will you wheel Dr. Fraser into one of our exam rooms, please?"

"Yes, Dr. Murdoch."

Sandra looked frustrated and Kody followed Dr. Coombs, who was wheeling Sandra into an exam room. Once the door was shut Sandra sat upright.

"This is silly. I'm not pregnant. I'm infertile. I can't have children."

Dr. Coombs said nothing as she prepared the test.

"You're going to humor Dr. Murdoch and get a blood test. You might not be pregnant, but maybe he can figure out why you've been sick for the last couple of weeks," Kody said.

"How did you know?" Then she shot Megan a look.

"I'm sorry, Dr. Fraser. Dr. Murdoch requested it." Megan bit her lip as she tied the tourniquet around Sandra's arm.

"Fine." Sandra lay back and closed her eyes.

He had this strange feeling that the test was going to be positive and he didn't know quite what to think about that. Of course, if she was, he'd love the child, there was no question about that, but he wasn't sure that he could marry her.

How would they raise this kid together?

And, this set back a lot of his plans. Again. *It's your child.*

Yeah, he could do anything for his child. The only thing that upset him was the thought he wouldn't see this child every day as he saw Lucy.

He watched as Dr. Coombs did the blood work and when she left, when they were finally alone in the room, he let out the breath he had been holding.

"I can't believe I fainted," Sandra murmured. "And I can't believe half the hospital will now be whispering and speculating that I'm pregnant."

"I don't think Dr. Coombs or Dr. Murdoch will say anything," Kody said. "Any time that I've dealt with them they've been professional."

Sandra sat up. "It's not them, but the orderlies."

"Ah," Kody said. "Well, you can't be pregnant, can you? I mean, we didn't use anything…but you said you couldn't have kids."

"I can't be." Sandra sighed. "I couldn't get pregnant naturally. My fertility doctor said I had unexplained infertility. He didn't know why I couldn't get pregnant and if I did through IVF, he didn't know why I miscarried the baby before I even knew I was pregnant. I tried everything with my ex-husband. I can't get pregnant. Not the traditional way."

His heart sank as he thought about the cancer that Jenny had. How they didn't even know until it was too late. When she got sick and they sat in a doctor's office, thinking they were going to have another baby and finding out that Jenny had advanced ovarian cancer instead.

He'd made his peace that there wasn't going to be any other child but Lucy, but that anxious thought about cancer, the horror of what happened to Jenny came rushing back. The thoughts of Sandra having cancer made him sick.

"Does cancer run in your family?" he asked quietly.

"I don't know." She sighed. "I was adopted, as you know, and I haven't had the guts to find out who my birth parents were and find out my genetic makeup."

"I thought all doctors did that?" he asked.

"I had great adoptive parents who loved me and, with all the infertility stuff, I never thought to look. I should. Perhaps that would explain why I couldn't have a child, but I wasn't really thinking about that back then.

"Why are you asking about cancer?"

"Jenny thought she was pregnant again and it was ovarian cancer."

"Way to think positive." She sighed. "I'm sorry. I understand your worry."

"I'm sorry too." He scrubbed a hand over his face. "I doubt it is that. Sorry for projecting my worry onto you."

She buried her head in her hands. "I just hope they find out what it is so I can get back to work. Ever since the flash flood, nothing has been the same."

"I wanted to talk to you about that," he said.

"Oh?"

"I haven't been purposely avoiding you, if that's what you were thinking. I'm on a different rotation. I'm on night shifts now. I started that rotation a couple days after the flood and I knew that was my rotation before…" He trailed off. "Before the cabin."

"Thanks. I haven't been avoiding you either. I've just been so sick during the day and a bit better at night, but tonight I started my shift with a junkie who smelled like garbage and cannabis, which made me retch. Then the appendectomy patient, when he started throwing up and I just lost all of my control." She swallowed hard. "Ugh, just thinking about it."

"Don't make yourself sick again," he said gently.

"Right." She chuckled. "I can't believe I fainted."

"Neither can I. You scared me."

"I'm glad you were there." She reached out and held his hand. "You don't have to stay."

"Yeah, I do. It's no problem. We're friends, right?" Even though he wanted to be more than friends. He wanted to tell her that he hadn't been able to stop thinking about her since that night in the cabin.

He wanted more from her; he just wasn't sure he could give her what she deserved.

He wasn't sure he could open his heart for her.

Sandra deserved so much better than only half his heart.

"Of course we're friends." She leaned against him and he sat down next to her.

"Don't puke on me, though, okay?" he teased.

Sandra laughed. "No promises."

"You really have a wonderful laugh. I like this side of you."

"What side is that? Vomiting, fainting, vertigo doctor?"

"Relaxed. Yourself." Just as she'd been that night in the cabin. She wasn't holding herself back. She wasn't hiding who she was to keep people at a distance, as she usually did.

She smiled at him weakly. "I haven't been myself in a long time."

There was a knock at the door and Dr. Murdoch came in, his expression serious. "I have your results, Dr. Fraser."

Kody stood up and held Sandra's hand. He hoped it wasn't cancer and he had a moment of panic, standing there waiting for the results.

"I'm sorry, Mrs. Davis, but you have stage four ovarian cancer, with metastases to the liver, lungs and pancreas. I'm so very sorry."

Kody shook that thought away. Well, whatever it was he was here for her. She was alone and needed him.

"What is it, Dr. Murdoch?" Sandra asked.

"Congratulations, Dr. Fraser, but you are

indeed pregnant. About eight weeks along, I'd say, but we'll do an ultrasound to be sure."

And Kody suddenly felt as if *he* was going to faint.

CHAPTER FIVE

PREGNANT?

Sandra wasn't quite sure she heard what Dr. Murdoch was saying. She blinked a couple of times, because she felt as if suddenly she were in some kind of alternative reality. She'd been told countless times she would never get pregnant unassisted.

And the couple of times she had got pregnant with IVF she'd lost the baby before she'd even known she was pregnant.

She'd never carried a baby past six weeks. Ever. She'd only ever conceived via IVF and now Dr. Murdoch was saying she was eight weeks pregnant!

"Pardon? What did you say?" she asked him again.

"You're pregnant. Your blood test confirmed elevated levels of the hormone HCG, which corresponds with a gestational age of about eight weeks. I'm going to get the ultrasound ready and we'll see what we can find." Dr. Murdoch left the room.

"Did he just say…?" Kody let go of her hand and ran his hands through his hair, making his usually neat black hair stand up on end. "Did he just say you're pregnant?"

"I think I'm going to be sick." Her stomach was turning, and she began to panic. It was all too much to take in and she couldn't quite believe it.

It was like a dream come true, but not in the way she expected at all.

Kody grabbed a kidney bowl and Sandra threw up in it, while Kody held back her hair. Once she was done, he took it away and then handed her a paper towel. She lay back down and tears stung her eyes.

"How can I be pregnant?" she whispered.

"Well…" Kody teased.

She sat up and slapped his arm. "This is no time for jokes!"

"Who's joking?" Kody said, astonished.

"What am I going to do?" She'd spent so

long trying to get pregnant, she'd lost pregnancies she hadn't even known about and had been through some painful procedures and nothing had taken. And if it had, it had never lasted long. She'd been so disappointed and heartbroken so many times. And there was no reason for her unexplained infertility. She had a bit of post-traumatic stress from it all.

She'd resigned herself to never having a baby and now, after one night with Kody, she was pregnant.

It almost seemed unbelievable. She didn't believe it. It was probably a phantom pregnancy or something. There was no way she could be pregnant.

Dr. Murdoch returned with the ultrasound. He dimmed the lights and wheeled it over to Sandra.

"Lift up your scrub shirt—you know the jelly will be cold?" Dr. Murdoch stated in his matter-of-fact way.

"I know, Burt." Sandra tucked the towel into the waist of her pants and pulled up her shirt. She was hoping that Dr. Murdoch would find something with the ultrasound, because otherwise she would have to make an appointment for a vaginal ultrasound with her OB/GYN because there was no way she was having Burt Murdoch perform that test on her tonight.

She watched the screen intently.

"Ah, there it is." Dr. Murdoch smiled at her. "That little dot, with the flickering. Do you see it?"

Sandra peered closely and could make out what looked like a little bean or something and the subtle flicker of a heart, fluttering away. It was a fully formed, tiny fetus. She knew by eight weeks that toes and fingers were being formed. She began to cry, covering her mouth. She could hardly believe it. It was true: there was a baby in there.

Her pregnancies had never gone this far. She had never seen the heart flicker and flutter like that, so she couldn't stop the tears from coming.

"So my original prediction of gestational age is correct. You're eight weeks along. Congratulations." Dr. Murdoch flicked off the machine and wiped her belly. "I take it Mr.

Davis is the father, since he seems to be a bit shell-shocked as well."

Kody nodded. "Yes. Yes. I am."

"Congratulations to the both of you. I'll leave you alone, but, Sandra, make an appointment with your OB/GYN fast. If what you say about your past fertility history is correct, you're a high-risk pregnancy. You can't work long hours in the ER if you want to keep this baby," Burt warned.

Dr. Murdoch left and Sandra let it all sink in. He was right. There was no way she could work now, but how the heck was she going to support herself or the baby? And she didn't expect anything from Kody. She could take care of herself. She always had since her parents' death.

She was going to have to go on light rotation. Maybe work in the clinic so she could support herself and the baby.

If it lasts.

There was a part of her that was terrified of the stark reality that this pregnancy might not last and she couldn't get too attached.

"You're pregnant," Kody said, a bit dumbfounded.

"Yeah," she responded dryly. "I was told this would never happen and, really, it might not last."

His brow furrowed and he frowned. "Why would you say that?"

"I've never had a pregnancy last long."

"Think positive."

"That's easy for you to say. You've never lost a child!"

He instantly regretted the words when he said them. She was right: he'd never lost a child. He'd lost Jenny, but Lucy was still with him. The only thing that came close to what Sandra was feeling, or felt, was before the cancer diagnosis, when they'd thought Jenny had been pregnant and it had turned out to be stage four ovarian cancer.

They had thought they were expanding their family. He'd got used to the idea of another baby, but then it had been cancer, so, even though it wasn't the same depth of loss that Sandra had experienced, he was no stranger to pain.

He was no stranger to the hope of a new baby, only to have it taken away.

"I'm sorry, but I tend to think positive." Kody helped her stand up. "I think you should go home."

"I suppose so, but my patients…"

"There are other doctors that can take care of your patients. Until you see your OB/GYN you're going to go home and rest. I can have Robbie drive the rig back and I'll drive you home." It was a statement rather than an offer. He *was* going to drive her back home and make sure she was okay. She might not need him, but, after all, this was his baby too.

"And what about your daughter?"

"She's with her grandparents for the weekend. I was working back-to-back night shifts and my sister couldn't watch her. She's fine. I can take you home and make sure you're comfortable."

And he was pretty sure they had a lot to talk about.

He was still in shock that she was pregnant. There were a lot of things he'd been expecting about the possibility of seeing Sandra again. Since their night together he hadn't been able to stop thinking about her. And he'd realized he missed seeing her.

He'd been hoping they would have dinner and talk; her fainting because she was pregnant with his child was not one of the possibilities that he'd imagined. This was the furthest thing from his wildest dreams.

Sandra got to her feet and he held her steady. She was still a bit dizzy; he could tell by the way she was moving.

"Maybe I should get you a wheelchair?" he offered.

She glared at him. "I'm perfectly capable of walking to the attendings' lounge, to collect my things from my locker and walk out of this hospital."

"You're sure?" he asked. "It seems like you still have some vertigo."

"Yes."

Kody wasn't so sure. "I'm going to tell Robbie that I'm taking you home. I'll meet you outside the attendings' lounge in a few minutes, okay?"

Sandra nodded and made her way out of the exam room.

Kody tried to smooth down his hair when he caught a glimpse of it standing on end in the mirror. How was he going to tell Robbie the reason why he was taking Dr. Sandra Fraser home? He hadn't told anyone what had happened between him and Sandra, because it wasn't anyone else's business, but people were going to find out sooner or later.

They were going to find out about their stolen night of passion in that cabin when they'd been stranded from the flooding.

Robbie was loitering at the charge station and talking to his girlfriend. He straightened when he saw Kody.

"Whoa, what happened? Did the patient die?" Robbie asked.

"No, he's fine… It's Dr. Fraser."

"Oh, what did she do now?" Robbie asked.

"I'm going to drive her home. She's really not well and she has no one to help her. I just want to make sure she gets home okay. Are you okay to take the rig back to the station?"

"Sure."

"Thanks, Robbie." Kody turned and walked back toward the attendings' lounge, relieved that had gone better than he'd thought it would. He'd thought Robbie would question him, because Robbie had always teased him about having a crush on Sandra.

Which wasn't a lie.

He did. And their one stolen night had only intensified his feelings for her, but they had both made it clear that night it was only to be a one-time thing.

This pregnancy just complicated a lot of things.

Sandra was sitting outside the lounge and looked annoyed.

"You ready?" he asked.

"You're sure about this?" she asked.

"Positive. You can't drive yourself and you need to get home and rest."

Sandra nodded. "Fine. I'm not happy about it, but fine."

Kody chuckled and followed her out of the hospital to the parking lot. She led him to her new SUV. It was cherry red and was a definite upgrade from the one he'd rescued her from.

"That's an improvement to your old SUV," he said as she handed him the keys.

"Yes. I'm happy with it, but I do miss my old SUV. That vehicle got me from California to Texas. It had sentimental value."

Kody opened her door and made sure she was seated and then took his spot in the driver's seat. He had to adjust the seat because she was only five foot eight and he was six-one. He needed a little bit more legroom.

He adjusted the mirrors and then started the ignition.

"You'll have to remind me where you live again. I have a vague idea of what direction to head in."

"Just follow the GPS." She punched in something and a map showed up on the console, directing him to her home.

"Cool!"

"It is…" She trailed off and then sighed.

"Kody, I want you to know if I thought there was any inkling that I could get pregnant I would've asked for protection or not given in to the passion I was also feeling."

He nodded. "I understand and I would've protested too. I'm sorry for my part in it."

"I'm not sorry that I'm pregnant. I'm worried about losing the baby, but it's something I've wanted for a long time. It's just not how I pictured it."

"Me neither." Then he cleared his throat. "I mean, I thought I wouldn't have any more children. I didn't ever want to get married again after losing Jenny. It was never in the plans to settle down again. It was just going to be Lucy and me. I am happy about the baby, though."

"I'm not asking you to marry me," Sandra said gently.

And he was embarrassed for implying that she expected a proposal from him. He hadn't expected that from her. He knew that she was dealing with her own demons, her divorce and unsuccessful fertility treatments.

"I never thought you were," he said. "I'm

sorry for implying it, but I want you to know that it's my baby too and I'm going to help in any way that I can."

"I appreciate that." Her voice trembled. "I just... I don't think it will last. They never do."

"Okay, but let's take it one day at a time. When you get home, leave a message with your OB/GYN and see if you can get in tomorrow afternoon. I'll take you to that appointment and we'll get things checked out. Don't focus on the future, but one day at a time."

"That's hard for me to do. As a surgeon—especially a trauma surgeon—I have to think fifteen steps ahead. I always have to look toward the inevitable."

"I respect that. Paramedics and first responders do too, but, for now, let's just take it one day at a time. Baby steps."

"Ha-ha...good pun," she said dryly, and he laughed.

"Not intended, but, yes, I suppose that is *pun*-derful." He winked.

Sandra groaned and then laughed. "Well,

until I pass out of the danger zone, I don't want to tell anyone. I know that you'll eventually need to talk to your daughter, but… I would hate to disappoint her or upset her needlessly if this doesn't pan out."

Kody nodded. "I agree. We'll keep it to ourselves for now."

He really didn't know how he was going to tell Lucy. Lucy didn't remember Jenny, not really, and he knew that she would be thrilled to have a little brother or sister, but it was Jenny's parents. They still grieved their daughter and he couldn't imagine starting a family, a life, with someone who wasn't Jenny.

It would break Myrtle's and Ted's hearts and he couldn't do that to them.

He wasn't sure what he was going to tell them.

Jenny might have told him to move on after she died, but he hadn't, and he wasn't sure that he could. He was kicking himself for giving in to that moment of temptation, because he liked Sandra Fraser, and if things had been different she was definitely the type of woman he would be interested in.

She reminded him of Jenny in some ways and other ways not at all, but he liked that about her. There were so many admirable qualities about Sandra Fraser.

She's off-limits. Remember?

And he had to keep reminding himself of that, but then there was the baby and he had to do right by Sandra and his unborn child.

No matter how conflicted his heart was.

His child came first.

Sandra was really glad that the cleaning lady had come through and Kody's first impression of her home wasn't going to be of a jungle of stuff.

Not that she had a lot of stuff, but still. She wasn't always the most organized, even on the best of days.

She unlocked the door and her body relaxed, because all she wanted to do was sleep, but she had to let Kody in to use her phone or at the very least wait for a cab or his sister to come and pick him up.

Although, he could take her car and if he promised to come back and get her the next day for her OB/GYN appointment, then he wouldn't have to wait around, but she had a feeling that she wouldn't be able to push Kody off tonight.

They had a lot to talk about.

She had felt a little embarrassed when he'd brought up the subject of not wanting to marry again and she hoped that he didn't think that was what she expected, because that was far from the truth. She didn't expect him to pop the question; she didn't want to get married.

There was no way she wanted to open her heart up to a mess like that again.

Who says marrying Kody would be a mess?

He was nothing like Alex. Alex had been just as charming as Kody, but it was different. Kody was a different kind of charming than Alex was. When she'd first met Kody she'd thought his charm labeled him as something he wasn't and nothing could be further from the truth. She'd been wrong about Kody.

Kody was genuine and Alex was not supportive. She knew that now.

Still, Kody was off-limits. She'd promised herself that she was never going to get married again. It was just going to be her, and now…well, it was hard for her to even think about it. It was hard for her even to begin to hope that it would work out.

She couldn't let herself think about it.

She'd been disappointed so many times before.

"So this is your place?" he asked as she opened the door and he followed in behind her.

"Yes, I got it at a fairly decent price. It was pretty abandoned and run-down when I bought it. I took a couple of months off when I first moved to Austin and did some of the work myself, but then realized that I suck at home renovations and hired people."

Kody chuckled. "So what did you actually do in here?"

"I did lay down the vinyl plank flooring. It was easy, though." She shut her front door and locked it.

Kody squatted and touched her floor. "Huh, I thought it was wood. Vinyl plank flooring is something I've never heard of."

"It's waterproof. Good for floods. Not that I've had any experience with that."

They both laughed at that and then an awkward silence fell between them.

"Can I get you something to drink?" she asked.

"I'm good."

"You must be hungry, though. You just got off shift."

"I am that. How about you? Are you hungry? You have to keep your strength up."

Sandra was going to say no, but then her stomach betrayed her. "I guess that I am."

"Do you have any eggs? I can make an omelet or some scrambled eggs with toast."

"I do." She led Kody into the kitchen, flicking on the lights and opening the fridge, but her head began to spin and Kody's arms went around her, steadying her. They were strong and made her feel safe.

They made her feel secure.

Don't get used to it.

If she lost the baby, Kody wouldn't be so attentive. And she'd be alone again. She had to prepare herself for that and not get attached.

"You okay?" he asked gently. "You started to sway."

"It was the scent of all that food. It was a bit overwhelming."

"You sit down. I can find my way around your kitchen and I'm going to make some ginger decaf tea. Something my grandmother always made when Sally and I were kids and our stomachs were feeling a bit wonky."

"I'd like that." Sandra sat down at her kitchen table. It was a booth seat with a large table, and it overlooked a large picture window out into the meadow. Of course, right now all she could see was darkness, but there was a pink tinge to the sky and the sun would be rising right in front of her.

Kody was rifling through her cupboards and soon had everything started. The smell of butter melting in the pan for the scrambled eggs didn't make her stomach protest and whatever tea he was brewing smelled divine.

She was looking forward to partaking.

The toaster popped and Kody set a piece of toast on a plate, then spooned out yellow fluffy eggs on top and set it down in front of her with a fork and knife.

"I'll be back with the tea," he announced. He poured the fragrant tea into a mug and set it in front of her.

"Mmm…it smells so good."

He smiled, pleased, and returned to sit next to her with his plate of eggs and toast and mug of tea for himself.

"I used to make this…" He trailed off.

"You can tell me about Jenny. I promise, it's okay. I know that you loved her, and I want you to feel comfortable talking about her to me." Which was true. And she was curious about her.

"I appreciate that." There was a gentle timbre to his voice, and she knew that he valued it.

"So, you made this for your late wife? Did she have morning sickness?"

"The worst, but this meal used to calm her stomach down," he said.

Sandra took a sip of the tea. "That's wonderful."

"Something my grandma learned from her mother and so on and so on. I learned a lot of wilderness medicine from my grandmother. She was full-blood Cherokee and even though she had to hide what she was learning from a lot of people, she still learned it, nonetheless. She didn't want to lose the knowledge, so I tried to learn what I could from her before she died."

"What else did you learn?"

"Brewing cedar leaves can help with iron deficiency, as well as other things, or at least that's what my grandmother told me. I don't know if there's scientific proof, but that's what she did."

"Good to know. It must be nice to have that kind of knowledge passed down to you. I know next to nothing about my biological parents."

"What about your adoptive parents?" Kody asked.

Sandra smiled as she thought about them. "They were both fifty when they adopted me. They were older, but they were the best parents a girl could ask for. They encouraged me to pursue medicine and taught me to stick up for myself and fight back. They taught me my gender didn't define me."

And she was sad thinking about that, because before she'd met Alex she had been a strong woman. She'd learned to speak up, to think for herself. And then slowly, over time, she was letting Alex speak for her. He became her voice, even though her mother had told her not to let that happen.

And then she'd struggled to have a child and Alex had questioned her as a woman.

When had she let her life spiral out of control? Even if she wanted to stop the tears from flowing, she couldn't. She broke down.

Kody wrapped an arm around her and just held her. It was exactly what she needed in that moment and she was glad that she hadn't sent Kody home.

They might not be together, but they were in this together and she appreciated his support. Even if a part of her was telling her not to trust him and that he'd leave her as soon as it got rough. Just as Alex did.

"I knew that my eggs were good, but I didn't think that they were so earth-shattering to bring about tears!" he teased gently, holding her.

Sandra started to laugh and wiped away the tears. "Yeah, that's it."

Kody smiled at her and then looked up at the window, whistling as the sun came up over the meadows, the foothills a black silhouette. Her favorite time of day, dawn.

"That's a beautiful view. I am envious of your land. You got a good piece out here."

"Thanks," she sighed. "I think I need some sleep, though. Do you want to take my car to get home?"

"I don't need to go home. Lucy is safe with my in-laws. If you don't mind me crashing on your couch, I'd like to stay. I want to make sure that you're okay."

She should tell him to go, that she was fine, but she was glad that he was staying after all. She could use a friend tonight, even if a part of her was telling her it was a bad idea.

That she should run, but she wanted him to be here. She didn't want to be alone tonight. It was nice to have someone who cared about her for a change.

"I would like that."

CHAPTER SIX

HER PHONE BUZZING woke her up out of deep sleep.

Sandra grabbed her phone and answered it. "Hello?"

"Sandra? This is Dr. Ohe."

"Jocelyn, thank you for getting back to me." Sandra tried to wipe the sleep from her eyes so that she could focus and talk to her OB/GYN with a clear head. She couldn't remember the last time she had slept so soundly. After she'd made sure Kody was settled, she'd gone to bed and couldn't even remember her head touching the pillow.

"No problem. Burt Murdoch filled me in when I got in this morning about what happened last night. Do you think you can come back here in about an hour? I want to run some tests and check you out myself."

"Sure. Sure. I was just sleeping, but I can get there." Sandra stifled a yawn.

"Good. With your medical history, I want to make sure that everything is okay and that you're okay. Does the father know?"

"Yes…" She sighed. "The father is the paramedic Kody Davis."

"Oh! Will he come in too?" Sandra could hear the surprise in Jocelyn's voice. A lot of people at the hospital were familiar with Kody. He was well liked, where she didn't have too many friends, but Jocelyn had been sympathetic when her medical file was sent over from San Diego.

"Yeah, he will. He's asleep on my couch."

There was a small chuckle. "Okay. I'll see you in an hour."

"Thanks, Jocelyn." Sandra ended the call and then got up, carefully because she was still feeling a bit woozy. She could hear clanging around in the kitchen and knew that Kody was up. She padded to the bathroom and wasn't sick, which was a bonus. She got dressed and tidied up. Kody was in the kitchen and making what smelled like tea.

"Good morning!" he said brightly when he saw her.

"Good morning. How did you sleep?" she asked.

He rubbed the back of his neck and made a face. "Not the best, but I've had worse."

"I'm sorry. I should've offered you my bed, or at the very least finish off the guest bedroom and put a bed in there."

"No worries. I heard your phone. Was that your OB/GYN?" he asked.

She nodded. "She wants to see us in an hour. So I'm hoping that's okay with you."

"Yeah. That's fine. Do you want to grab some breakfast on the road?"

"Sure, but I'm going to take some more of that tea in a travel mug if I can." The tea had calmed down her stomach immensely. It tasted good and kept the nausea away; it was a win-win.

"Of course." Kody opened a cupboard and pulled down a travel mug, filling it with the ginger tea that he'd made her last night. The tea that seemed to work miracles and helped ease her morning sickness.

Once the travel mug was filled, they got their stuff together and headed out in her SUV back toward downtown Austin and Rolling Creek General Hospital. Only this time they weren't headed to the emergency department, which was unusual for them. They were headed to the main entrance and Kody cursed under his breath when he accidentally took a wrong turn and headed down the ambulance ramp, as he was so used to doing when he was driving his rig.

It made Sandra chuckle, because she was so used to driving down this way to park in the staff parking that was closer to the emergency department in the large sprawling hospital. Although she never walked through the main emergency room admitting doors before a shift—every ER doctor and nurse knew that was bad luck.

So it was surreal to walk through the front doors of Rolling Creek as a patient and head up to the OB/GYN floor.

When she got there, the waiting room was full of pregnant women, some with small kids, and it was a bit much to take in.

She felt so out of place, as if she didn't belong, that she took a step back. Kody put his hand on the small of her back. It was reassuring and a comfort.

Don't get used to it.

Still, she couldn't pull away from his touch. It was comforting and she could definitely use some of that right now.

She was terrified that everything that'd happened last night was just a dream and she'd go in there to find out she wasn't pregnant.

"It's okay," he whispered in her ear, as if reading her mind.

She nodded and took a seat, with Kody sitting next to her. She was trying to be inconspicuous, but she felt as if everyone was looking at her.

"Dr. Fraser?" the nurse called out.

Sandra got up and followed the nurse into the exam room. Kody lingered in the door.

"She's going to need to do a vaginal ultrasound. How about you wait in the waiting room and I'll give you a call when the doctor has done her exam?" the nurse suggested to

Kody, who looked a bit relieved not to have to stay in the room.

Sandra was relieved too.

They might have been intimate, but they weren't to that level of intimacy.

Yet.

And probably never will be.

She shook that thought away.

"I'll be in the waiting room, Sandra." He left the exam room and the nurse shut the door.

At least she had a moment to collect her thoughts and prepare herself for the worst and think of what to tell Kody, if what she thought was going to happen happened.

Come on. What's going on?

Kody resisted the urge to get up and pace. Logically, he knew that the test would take a while, he was a paramedic and had the basic grasp of how medical tests worked, but still, it felt as if it were going on forever.

He glanced at the clock. And it seemed as if time hadn't moved forward at all. He hoped Sandra was okay. He hoped the baby was okay.

The baby.

He was still in shock about that. He was happy and he'd love the child just as much as Lucy, but another baby had never been in his plans. He'd never thought it would happen again.

Of course, a lot of things in his life didn't exactly go according to plan.

What was supposed to be a one-time thing with Sandra had now turned into a lifetime.

Even if they weren't together, they were both this child's parents. They both were bonded forever by their child.

If she wants you around.

And that thought sobered him. What if Sandra moved on with someone else? What if someone else was raising his child? What if Sandra moved away from Austin and took his child with her?

The thought of all those things scared him.

He glanced at the clock again.

I think it's going backward!

"Mr. Davis, they're ready for you now," a nurse said, coming into the waiting room.

"Thanks." Kody got up and followed the nurse down to the exam room.

When he walked into the room, Sandra was lying there with tears in her eyes. His heart sank to the soles of his feet.

Oh, no.

"Sandra…" He trailed off. He didn't know what to say.

"No, it's fine," she said. "It's still there."

He let out a sigh of relief. "Oh. I thought…"

"Sorry." She smiled. "I had prepared myself for disappointment. I hadn't prepared myself for good news."

He laughed.

Dr. Jocelyn Ohe came in then. "Ah, good to see you again, Kody."

"How do you two know each other?" Sandra asked.

"He delivered my baby when I was stuck in the back of a cab." Jocelyn gave Kody a hug.

"How is your little boy? What did you call him again?" Kody asked, teasing.

Jocelyn laughed. "You know I called him

Kody, and Kody Jr. is fine, thank you. He's five now."

"Five!" Kody whistled. "He must be getting into trouble."

"Hey!" Sandra said quickly. "I'm sorry to interrupt this reunion, but what's going on, Jocelyn?"

Jocelyn took a seat and pulled up the imaging. "Dr. Murdoch was right, you're about eight weeks along, given the dates of your last menstrual cycle and the time of conception."

"And everything looks good?" Kody asked as he stared at that tiny little blob on the screen. The little clump of cells that was in the process of forming rudimentary organs. The little person growing limbs, toes and eyelids, if he remembered all those baby books he'd read when Jenny was pregnant.

His little person.

His and Sandra's.

"So far," Jocelyn said. "But given your history, Sandra, from your doctor in San Diego, I'm going to tell the chief of surgery that you are officially on maternity leave. You can't be working. You need to take it easy."

"So bed rest?" she asked.

"No. Not bed rest, but take it easy. No heavy lifting or anything. Until we get through this first trimester, you're high risk. And really, I want you to get past twenty-nine weeks' gestation. Any baby can be born prematurely after twenty-nine weeks' gestation and has a good chance of survival. Twenty-five weeks is pushing it...under twenty-five weeks is touch and go. I won't lie. I'm worried that you will deliver early."

Kody scrubbed a hand over his face. "Is there anything I can do, Dr. Ohe?"

"Make sure she rests. Do you two live together?" Jocelyn asked.

"No, we're not an item," Sandra said quickly. "It was a one-night thing. It was supposed to be a one-night thing."

"Oh," Jocelyn said, raising her eyebrows.

"I can take care of her. She doesn't live that far out of the city and lives close to my late wife's parents. I can check in on her," Kody said.

"I can take care of myself," Sandra said stubbornly.

"You fainted and you've been sick and dizzy," Kody said firmly. "Did you tell the doctor about that?"

"She did," Jocelyn said, standing. "I want to see you back here in two weeks. If you have any pain, call me and have me paged. Call Kody or an ambulance, just get here, okay?"

Sandra nodded. "Okay."

"Good. I'll see you in two weeks." Jocelyn left the room.

Kody let out the breath he hadn't realized that he'd been holding in and sat down on the wheelie stool that Dr. Ohe had been occupying.

"Well, I think you should move in with me and Lucy."

Sandra's eyebrows shot up. "What?"

"It's the only solution to make sure that you're taken care of."

"Kody, you're not thinking rationally here. We're not in a relationship, and do you really want to confuse your daughter? What would you tell her?"

"Right." Kody ran his hand through his hair. "I was just thinking of that baby. Our baby. I want to take care of you, Sandra. I'm the one that got us in this mess."

She smiled at him warmly. "It takes two to tango. I appreciate you wanting to help me, and I'll gladly accept any and all help, but I'm okay. I can take care of myself. I have been for a while."

"I'm going to give you my cell and you're going to call me whenever you need me. It's only a twenty-minute drive from my place to yours."

"That sounds good and I'll give you mine. We're in this together, whether we like it or not."

Kody nodded. "Let me take you home and then I can get a cab back to my place."

"I can drive, Kody. I feel good. How about we go have some lunch, figure out what we're going to tell people and how we're going to do this and how to break it to Lucy? Or, more importantly, when. I would hate to break her heart if we tell her too soon."

"When's the first trimester over officially?" he asked.

"Twelve weeks is the end of the first trimester."

"We'll tell her then. That's only a few weeks away."

Sandra nodded, but worried her bottom lip as she stood up. "I've never made it to twelve weeks. I've never even made it this far."

"We'll take it one day at a time. Remember."

She nodded. "One day at a time. Right."

They walked out of the hospital prenatal clinic together. Kody didn't know what to say; he was still having a hard time trying to process all the emotions he was feeling and there was no one but Sandra to talk to.

Lucy was too young to understand, and he didn't want to tell Myrtle and Rick. Not yet, because he felt so damn guilty about it.

You shouldn't feel guilty.

He shook that thought away, because he did. He really felt guilty.

As if he was betraying Jenny, because he cared about Sandra and he cared about their baby. He wanted to help her any way he could. He wanted to be there for her, but how could he be there for her when he didn't even know how he was feeling?

"You could do me a favor right now," Sandra said, interrupting his self-deprecating thoughts.

"What's that?"

"How about some lunch? I'm starving and I haven't felt like eating this much in a long time. It must be your grandmother's tea."

"Sure."

"Do you know any good places in Austin? I haven't been exploring much, so I don't know many restaurants."

"I do. Do you think you can handle some barbecue, or is that too much?"

She tilted her head to one side. "We can give it a try."

The barbecue place that he was thinking of was down near Lady Bird Lake. It overlooked a particularly nice vantage point of the lake and today was a calm, warm day, so they opted to enjoy their lunch on the restaurant's patio, so they could watch the paddleboarders out enjoying a sunny Saturday in Austin.

"I didn't know this lake was here," Sandra said, taking a sip of her iced tea, unsweetened, which Kody found slightly horrifying.

"Yeah, it's a pretty nice spot. What I'm more concerned about is how you can drink iced tea that's not sweetened. Yuck!"

"You know that iced tea in Canada is always sweetened?"

"I won't have a problem in Canada, then," Kody stated. "Why are we talking about Canada?"

"I just thought it was an interesting fact and I was trying to change the topic."

"I've never had anyone try to change a topic by talking about Canada with me."

She chuckled softly. "I just prefer my tea this way. I don't like overly sweet things."

"You like me," he teased.

She rolled her eyes but smiled. "You're a bit of a dork—you know that, don't you?"

"I've only ever heard my sister call me that."

"It must've been nice having a sibling growing up," she said wistfully. "I never did. I may have a biological half sibling or two out there, though."

"Why don't you obtain your adoption records?" he asked, curious.

"I don't know. I should, given the fact that I'm pregnant now. Even if I could just find out my medical history."

Kody nodded. "You should."

"I guess I never have because I loved my adoptive parents so much that it felt like I was cheating on them a bit if I tried to find out who my biological parents were."

He understood that, because that was what he was currently feeling about this whole baby situation. It felt as if he were cheating.

You're not, though.

"Well, at least get your DNA tested and see what things you might be at risk for inheriting or what our baby might be at risk for."

"You're right. I'll make an appointment with my general practitioner and get the blood work done."

"Or, you are a doctor, you could do it yourself?"

"I'm not going to draw my own blood." She rolled her eyes. "They only pull that kind of stunt on TV. I'll go to my doctor, thank you very much." She took another sip of her tea as they both watched the paddleboarders out on the lake. It was sunny and watching people stand and slowly paddle across the calm waters was kind of mesmerizing.

"So, have you ever tried paddleboarding?"

"Nah." He shook his head. "Doesn't appeal to me. It looks kind of boring."

"It's really fun," she said.

"You've done it?"

She nodded. "I'm from California. Of course I have. The best time was paddleboarding on Lake Tahoe—of course, that water is cold. You don't want to fall in."

"Really? It looks so warm."

"Well, if you find a shallow bay, but Tahoe is pretty deep and high in altitude, so it never really gets warm. Would you go swimming in some of the lakes in Alaska?" she teased.

"Yeah, probably not. I doubt they really warm up. Still, it was a dream of mine to go up there." He sighed. "Well, we all have unfulfilled dreams."

"And it's Lucy and your late wife's parents holding you back. And now me." He could hear the sadness in her voice.

"Hey, don't blame yourself. I made peace with my decision a long time ago. It was Jenny's and my dream to go to Alaska. That's not going to happen. When she got sick, I let it go."

"You still want to fly, though?" she asked.

"I do. One day I'll get my pilot's license. One day," he said wistfully, "I'll get some land and my own plane. It'll be nice."

"It sounds wonderful."

"I am envious of your property. It's perfect for an airstrip." He cleared his throat, hoping that she didn't think he was implying something, because he wasn't, and he didn't want to scare her off.

"It is lovely, but so large for one person." A blush tinged her cheeks.

"Soon there'll be two of you."

She smiled, her dark eyes twinkling. "I suppose so."

He reached out and took her hand. "I know so."

The food came then. Sandra had just ordered a cob of corn and a side of macaroni and cheese. Once they got to the restaurant she found she had no real desire to order any kind of protein, beyond the cheese in her macaroni. He just hoped that his steak wouldn't be off-putting to her.

"You're sure it's okay that I eat this in front of you? You seemed a bit green around the gills when we were inside ordering."

"I'm fine. I'm glad we're outside and in the fresh air." She wouldn't look at his plate of food, though.

"Me too."

They sat in silence, eating and watching the activity out on Lady Bird Lake. Usually when things went quiet between them there was an awkward tension, but Kody didn't sense any of that now. It was peaceful and nice to sit with her here, out on a patio and enjoying some good food.

"You know, even though I may not tell Lucy yet about the baby, I would like you to meet her," Kody said, breaking the silence.

"You want me to meet her?" she asked, stunned.

He nodded. "Yeah. I mean, she's going to wonder why we're hanging around together so much. She might as well meet you and when the time comes, we'll tell her about the baby. She'll be thrilled about that. She loves babies."

"Are you sure?" Sandra asked skeptically. "She may love babies, but it's one thing to love a stranger's baby and another the reality of a baby stealing away your father's attention, especially after she's had you all to herself for years."

"I never thought about it that way. Still, I'd like you to meet her."

"Okay. We can have dinner tomorrow. Your place?"

"Sure, that sounds good."

"What time?"

"Five is good. It's early, but she eats early and then I have to get her ready for school on Monday and try to sleep. You may be off work, but I'm still on nights."

Sandra winced. "Don't remind me. I hate that I'm not working. I love my job. I love teaching the residents and working in the emergency room."

"You like the fast pace?"

She nodded. "I do. When I was doing my surgical residency, I knew that was my specialty. I like thinking ten steps ahead. I liked thinking fast on my feet. It was thrilling. I'm going to miss it."

"I'm sorry for that, but once the baby comes, we'll work out a schedule to take care of him or her and you can go back to work."

"I know. We'll figure it out and the hospital has an excellent day care. I just don't know what I'm going to do with myself for the next thirty-two weeks, give or take."

"Or longer." He winked.

"What do you mean, longer?"

"First babies are known to be overdue."

Sandra groaned. "Sure. Low blow there, Mr. Davis. That wasn't cool at all."

CHAPTER SEVEN

SANDRA TOSSED AND turned that night.

Kody had gone back to his home and to his daughter and Sandra suddenly didn't like being all alone in her house. She couldn't stop worrying about this pregnancy.

She glanced at her phone. Kody had given her his number and told her to call or text whenever she wanted. She was trying her best not to do that.

The last thing she wanted to do was bother Kody when he was having some alone time with his daughter. She was the intruder. Also, she didn't want to rely on him.

Her emotions were all over the place, she knew that, but she couldn't go running to Kody every time she felt anxious about something.

Still, there was no one she could talk to. She didn't have any friends.

And whose fault is that?

She sighed, because she knew that it was her fault for shutting out everyone when she'd first moved here six months ago. She didn't want to get to know anyone. She didn't want to let anyone into her life.

She didn't want to be hurt again.

Alex had moved on and remarried. And then his new wife had got pregnant and she'd seen the look of pity in her colleagues' eyes. People who she'd thought were friends weren't. They pitied her for not getting pregnant and for not being woman enough for Alex. Whatever that meant.

She'd sworn that she wasn't going to make that mistake again when she came to Austin. So she'd put up walls and it had worked, until Kody showed up.

Sandra groaned and got out of bed. It was eight o'clock and too early to sleep. Her body was still on the night shift, which she had signed up to work for the next couple of weeks. Now her body wasn't sure what was going on.

She made her way to her living room and turned on the television, scrolling through her streaming service and trying to find something, anything, that could just be white noise in the background. Maybe some crazy reality show about people who were prepping for the end of the world or a home renovation show. She liked those.

There was a knock at her door, which startled her. She made her way carefully over to the peephole and was shocked to see Dr. Coombs standing on her porch holding a takeaway bag.

Sandra opened the door. "Dr. Coombs, what're you doing here?"

Megan shrugged. "I thought you could use a friend. Also, Kody texted me to check up on you. I'm the only one besides Dr. Murdoch and Dr. Ohe who knows what's going on."

Sandra was stunned and motioned for Megan to come inside. She shut the door.

"Wait, what about those orderlies?"

"Dr. Murdoch made sure they didn't say

a word, or they would lose their jobs. Burt knows how important your privacy is."

"I'll have to thank Burt later. Why don't you have a seat? I was just…going to watch something, but it's been so long since I actually turned on my television, I don't know what to watch."

"I brought some Chinese food. It's a cliché, I know, but when I was pregnant it was all I wanted to eat."

Sandra was surprised. "You have a baby?"

Megan blushed. "I did… I was young. I was a teenager and not ready to be a mother. I gave my baby up for adoption. She's in good hands and they send me updates all the time. It was an open adoption."

Sandra was so shocked. "I had no idea. I was adopted, but my adoption wasn't open. I have the option to open it now, but…"

Megan nodded. "I get it. It must be so hard."

"It is. You understand."

"All too well, but can we keep this between us? The whole hospital doesn't need to know."

"It's between us, Megan. I promise."

Megan smiled and nodded. "Are you hungry?"

"Very. I'll get some plates." Sandra went to the kitchen and grabbed everything they needed and brought it back. She hadn't expected Megan to come, but she was glad that she had, and she was glad that her prickly persona hadn't driven everyone away.

Sandra set the plates down on her coffee table. "Look, I want to apologize if I was ever too gruff to you or mean in any way."

Megan's eyes widened. "Dr. Fraser, you're one of the best trauma surgeons I have ever had the pleasure to work with. It's an honor to learn from you and I'm really sad that in my last years of residency I won't be working with you."

Sandra blushed. "I don't know what to say… Wait, I do. Don't call me Dr. Fraser here. Call me Sandra, and I'm very honored to be teaching you too. You have a promising career in trauma surgery, if you choose to accept it."

"I do. It's what I want to do."

"Why don't you fill me in on my appendectomy?"

They chatted about patients and Sandra gave her some advice on patient care while they ate the Chinese food. For that couple of hours Sandra forgot everything. All her anxiety and her worry melted away.

She'd always liked working with Megan and she viewed Megan as one of her top residents, but now she saw a friend and, even though it scared her, she liked it.

"So I don't mean to pry, but when did you and Kody Davis hook up?" Megan asked, smiling.

"I knew that someone was going to eventually ask that."

"Well, every time you two worked together the last six months it was like cats and dogs. He seemed to drive you crazy."

"He did…he does." Sandra chuckled. "I always found him attractive and, even if I hate to admit it, he's quite charming."

Megan nodded. "He is."

"How do you know Kody?" Sandra asked, trying to change the subject.

"I'll tell you how I know Kody, but first you have to tell me how it happened. Okay, maybe not all the details, but when?"

"The night of the flash flood. I guess it was a way to keep warm." Sandra began to laugh, and Megan joined in. "So, how do you know Kody outside of work?"

"I was friends with his late wife, Jenny."

Sandra's heart sank and did a flip-flop. "You knew Jenny? I thought they were from North Carolina?"

"So am I. I lived in the same town as Kody for one year when we were about fourteen. I went to his school and then my family moved away. I met Kody again when he and Jenny came to Austin. Jenny was a paramedic too and, when I first met them, I was a nurse studying and saving up for medical school. Then I did a palliative nursing rotation and sadly Jenny was in my care when she was dying."

"I was sorry to hear that she died. She seemed like a lovely person."

Megan nodded. "She was. What she saw in Kody I'll never know. He was such a hooligan when I knew him. Of course, most four-teen-year-old boys are."

Sandra cocked an eyebrow. "Oh, really? Do tell."

"I don't know if I should."

Sandra could tell by the mischievous glint in Megan's eyes that it wouldn't take much to get her to spill the beans about Kody. "I'm your boss...or was, so you have to tell me about the crazy stuff the father of my child did as a teenager."

Megan chuckled. "Well, there was this time he painted his body purple, and I mean every inch of his body purple, and streaked during homecoming."

Sandra started to belly laugh. She couldn't help it. "He streaked?"

Megan nodded. "Yep, so when I say I know Kody Davis, I mean I *know* Kody Davis."

They both laughed at that.

"I'm going to file that away for future use."

"Do, but he's going to kill me for telling that story." Megan glanced at her watch. "I'd better get going."

"Yeah, it's getting late. Thank you for coming. I wouldn't mind if you came again—perhaps I can help you study for your final boards?"

She wanted to do something and helping Megan study at least kept her foot in the medical world from the comfort of her own home.

"I would like that, Sandra. Perhaps I'll stop by Tuesday afternoon after my shift. We can go shopping or have a coffee somewhere."

"I'd like that." Sandra walked her out and made sure that Megan got in her car okay. When she drove away, Sandra shut the door.

Her plan when she came to Austin was to not make any friends and not get involved with another man she worked with.

She was terrible with making plans and sticking to them.

"I don't know what to make for dinner!"

Sally blinked a couple of times and looked at him as if he were insane. All she could do was stare at him as if he were crazy instead of helping him with dinner.

"What has got you all worked up?" she asked.

"I need to make something for dinner," Kody repeated.

"Okay, you've made dinner before." Sally followed him into the kitchen, her arms crossed, still staring at him as if he'd lost his mind. Maybe he had. He wanted Lucy to meet Sandra. It was important that they did meet, but now he wasn't so certain that this was the smartest plan.

Perhaps Sandra had been right, and it was too soon.

You're not telling Lucy she's going to be a sister, though.

Kody sat down at his table, which was currently littered with coloring books and glitter. In fact, when he lifted his hand, it was covered in a great blob of pink and silver glitter.

"Great, this stuff never comes out. It'll be everywhere."

Sally cocked an eyebrow and grabbed a wet wipe from the counter, handing it to him. "What is up with you? What has got you so damn skittish and freaked out?"

"I have a woman coming over to dinner to meet Lucy."

Sally grinned. "You have a date?"

"It's not a date!" he said firmly, trying to scour the glitter off his hands. "It's a dinner and I have no idea what to cook. Something that's bland. Something that's safe, so no sushi or anything raw or undercooked. No salmon from the ocean…"

Sally wrinkled her nose. "Something that's bland or not raw or sushi or salmon? Why would you do that? Is your date pregnant?"

Kody felt the blood drain from his face, and he couldn't look Sally in the eye. Sally sat down right in front of him and snapped her fingers in his face.

"You got this non-date woman pregnant?"

"Shh! Lucy doesn't know and we're not telling her yet. We need to take this slow. The lady in question has had troubles in the past with previous pregnancies and we're waiting until she's out of the first trimester."

Sally furrowed her brow. "Oh, my God, it's Dr. Fraser!"

"Why would you think that?"

"Because since you laid eyes on her you've been interested in her. I know, I'm not blind.

Plus, that morning after the flood..." Her eyes widened. "Oh, my God!"

"Shut up!" Kody admonished, craning his neck to make sure that Lucy was out of earshot. "You're not supposed to know, but secretly I'm glad you figured it out."

"When did this happen?"

"She's eight weeks along."

"So it was the flash flood! I knew it. That night you spent in the cabin, the way you two looked so guilty in the morning. Oh, my God. I can't believe this. Why didn't you use protection?"

"She said she couldn't get pregnant. She was infertile."

Sally rolled her eyes. "Well, that was a lie."

"She didn't do this for malicious reasons, Sally. She really thought she was infertile."

"Well, I'm excited. How involved are you going to be? Are you two an item?"

"No, we're not an item but we're going to raise the baby together, if that's what you're asking."

"Why aren't you two pursuing a relationship? You obviously both like each other."

Kody sighed. "It's complicated."

And it was. Although Sally would understand how he felt. She'd struggled with her own issues when she got divorced and Sally was in a much better place now. She was in a relationship with Ross and she was happy.

Kody envied her, but Sally didn't have kids.

Kody had Lucy, and Lucy took priority. And Sally also didn't have her in-laws living in the same city and still pretty much interwoven in her life, as he did. This whole thing was a disaster.

There was a part of him that wanted to move on and give it a try, but then there was a part of him that was too scared to try.

He ran his hands through his hair and groaned. "I don't know what to do. I could use some guidance."

Sally was laughing. "Well, how about I make up the dinner, something bland for someone who is having some morning sickness, and you take a shower?"

"Why?" he asked. "I already had one."

"You have pink glitter in your hair, my friend."

Crap.

He got up and saw that he did, indeed, have a streak of pink glitter in his black hair.

"Fine. You do the dinner and I'll try to wash this glitter out of my hair and if she shows up, you can't say a word about the baby. We promised that we wouldn't tell anyone else."

"I swear." Sally made a motion of zipping her lips, as she often did when they were kids. It'd annoyed him then too. "But I am happy. I'm really happy about this."

Kody smiled. "Yeah, me too."

When he came out of the shower, he could smell stuff cooking. Sally worked fast. He came into the kitchen when he was dressed and Lucy was helping Sally clean off the table, so they didn't have to dine on glitter.

"I have got to run, I'm needed at the station house, but there's chicken in the oven and vegetables and roast potatoes. I think that would be best for your friend." Sally glanced at Lucy with a side-eye.

"Thanks, Sweet Pea."

Sally nodded, kissed Lucy on the top of her head and left.

"Who's coming over for dinner, Daddy?" Lucy asked.

"A friend of mine from work. She's new to Austin. She's a doctor."

Lucy smiled and nodded but didn't take her eyes off her chore. "Sorry about the glitter. I forgot that it spilled."

"That's okay. You're helping to clean it up now and that's good. Hopefully there's none in my hair anymore."

Lucy glanced up and peered at the top of his head. "Just a bit. Can I go outside and play until the doctor gets here?"

"Sure."

Lucy got up from the table and he heard the back door open and shut. She was perfectly safe in his fenced backyard and he could see her from the kitchen window. It wasn't long before her neighborhood friend joined her, and they were playing in her little playhouse with their dolls.

He checked on dinner and Sally had a done a good job prepping something out of the hodgepodge of groceries he'd bought in a panic. There was nothing for him to do now but wait. So he decided to set the table.

It was busy work and it kept his mind off the fact that he was introducing a woman to Lucy. That he was introducing a woman he'd been intimate with, a woman he was interested in, to Lucy. He'd never done that before.

Lucy had met his friends before, though, and he was trying to approach this from the angle that he and Sandra were just friends, but try as he might he couldn't wrap his head around that, because he was attracted to Sandra.

He always had been.

And he'd made love with her. He'd thought about that night in the cabin often, ever since it happened, but he was so terrified about what it would mean to move on.

A knock at the door interrupted his thoughts and he could see Sandra standing on his porch through the screen door. She was holding what looked like a pie.

"Hey, Sandra. Come on in—the door's open."

Sandra opened the door and nervously stepped in. "I bought a pie on the way here."

"I thought you would've baked it," he teased.

"No. I'm the worst baker ever. My mom tried to show me numerous times, but it was a lost cause. I accidentally poisoned my dad once and sent him to the emergency room with acute stomach pains." She laughed nervously.

Kody took the pie. "How do you accidentally poison someone baking?"

"Ah, well, when your mother tells you to grease the pan it's best if you use lard instead of axel grease."

Kody laughed. "Good point. Come on in and sit down."

He took the pie to the kitchen and Sandra perched on the edge of his couch in the living room. She looked highly uncomfortable and nervous. He was glad he wasn't the only one feeling like that.

"Can I get you anything to drink?" he asked her from the kitchen.

"No, thank you."

He returned to the living room and sat next to her on the couch. They didn't say anything.

"Does Lucy know I'm coming?" she asked, breaking the silence.

"She does. I told her you were my friend."

"Naturally, and of course I am." Her eyes narrowed and she reached out to touch his hair. "Why do you have pink glitter in your hair?"

He groaned and ran his hand through his hair again. "Damn, I thought I got it all. Long story short I touched a glitter bomb on my table and then ran my hand through my hair in a moment of stress when I was trying to figure out what to make for dinner."

Sandra giggled. "Well, it suits you."

"Thanks. Do you want to go meet my glitter bomber? She's outside in the backyard, and then maybe we'll go sit on the front porch. I don't have chairs in the backyard of doom."

"Backyard of doom?" Sandra asked, getting up and following him.

"It's just full of outdoor toys and a play-house. It's a disaster really." He held open the back door and they walked out into his postage-stamp backyard. "Lucy, can you come out here for a moment and meet my friend Dr. Fraser?"

Lucy popped out of her play tent and came over to them.

"Lucy, this is Dr. Sandra Fraser, and, Sandra, this is my daughter, Lucy."

Lucy smiled up at Sandra. "Nice to meet you, Doctor. What kind of doctor are you?"

"I'm a trauma surgeon...or rather I operate on people who are really hurt in the emergency department."

"Cool, like people who get an arm chopped off or impaled or something?"

Kody was mortified. "Where did you learn about impaling?"

"Some boy at school was talking about something he saw on the internet. So, Dr. Fraser, have you dealt with that?"

Sandra's eyes were wide, and he could tell that she was trying very hard not to laugh at the little girl, dressed in a princess gown, asking her about impaling and lost limbs.

"I have," Sandra said. "Metal pole, right through his belly button."

"Cool! Did he survive?"

"Lucy! What has got into you?" Kody asked, astonished.

Lucy shrugged. "Aunt Sally tells me a bunch of stuff all the time."

"I need to have a talk with your aunt Sally, then," Kody muttered.

Sandra was laughing behind her hand. She was thoroughly enjoying this.

"He did survive, in fact, and he learned not to try and pass people on the road when you're not supposed to pass, especially when you're on a motorbike," Sandra said.

"Cool!"

"I think you should go back and play with your friend." Kody pushed his daughter off back toward her playhouse and shook his head as he led Sandra through the backyard gate and up the driveway to the front porch. "I don't know what's got into her. I've never heard her ask about stuff like that before in my life."

"Well, maybe she doesn't say it to you, but she obviously listens or talks to her aunt," Sandra said. "She seems fascinated, though, by it. I was fascinated by it all when I was about her age."

He cocked an eyebrow and pulled out a lawn chair for her. "So, you're telling me that you were interested in limbs and impalement?"

Sandra chuckled. "Okay, maybe not to *that* extent, but I was certainly interested to know how the body worked and what was going on inside. I'm wondering, too, if she didn't say those things for shock value because she's meeting a friend of her father's…who happens to be a female."

"Good point. I don't bring around many friends. She knows my partner, Robbie, and my best friend, Ross, who is dating Sally, but that's about it."

"How about Megan Coombs?"

Kody scratched his head. "Yeah, she knows Megan a bit, but not a whole lot. Megan was Jenny's nurse. How did you know that?"

"You sent her to check up on me." There was a twinkle in her eyes and his stomach sank.

"What. Did. She. Tell. You?"

Sandra leaned back and made a face as if she were trying to recall it, but he knew whatever Megan had told him was at the forefront of her mind. He'd forgotten, briefly, that Megan had been sort of privy to his crazy past life the one year they were in junior high school together before Megan moved away. When he'd been fourteen and dumb.

"Something about a streak?"

Kody scrubbed his hand over his face. "I'm going to kill her."

"You took an oath to do no harm!" Sandra stated, trying not to laugh.

"I did not! She did, but I didn't."

Sandra was laughing, belly laughs, and Kody couldn't help but join in.

"Please tell me you have a picture."

"Why do you want to see a picture of my bare butt, colored purple, streaking across the football field?" he asked, curious about her interest.

"I don't know. I guess it's a case of seeing is believing?"

"Trust me. It happened, and it took forever

to get all the paint out of every nook and cranny."

She shook her head, trying to tell him to stop, but she was laughing too hard.

"I'm glad that my pain brings you so much pleasure," he said dryly. "Didn't you do anything stupid when you were a teenager?"

"No, not *that* stupid, but I did go skinny-dipping. A lot."

"In the ocean?" he asked.

"Sometimes, but sometimes we'd drive up into the mountains and find a hot spring or something."

"Who is *we*?" he asked, feeling a slight twinge of jealousy.

She shrugged. "A group of friends. An old boyfriend or two. It doesn't seem like it, but I do have a bit of a wild side. Just that as a doctor, and the head of Trauma, I've learned to curb some of my wilder tendencies."

"That's a shame," he said huskily. "I wish I'd known that wild Californian girl."

Pink bloomed in her cheeks. "She's in here somewhere, but I don't think I'll be doing any kind of skinny-dipping or anything like that anytime soon."

"Right. Yeah, I guess when you become a parent you sort of have to grow up."

She nodded. "I suppose so."

"And there is a picture," he said, winking.

"Really?"

"Yeah, but it's just a blur and from the paper. My mother was so angry when she saw it. If I wasn't bigger than her, she probably would've tanned my hide."

"Did she often have to?"

He chuckled. "No, she just made it known that we'd be in a world of hurt."

Sandra chuckled and then she sniffed the air. "Is something burning?"

Oh. My. God. "The chicken!"

He dashed inside and saw the smoke billowing out from the oven. He opened the oven carefully and pulled out a blackened chicken, one that wasn't supposed to be blackened. The carrots matched the chicken, as did the potatoes.

He heard the window open behind him and coughing, as Sandra had followed him inside.

She was opening the kitchen windows to let in some air.

Lucy came in from the backyard.

"Whoa!" Lucy said. "What happened?"

"I burned the dinner Aunt Sally prepared for us," Kody mumbled, setting down the mess on the top of his stove and turning the oven off.

"It was a valiant effort," Sandra said, trying not to cough.

"I promised you dinner," Kody said. "This is not how I planned today to go."

"Well, how about we go out somewhere?" Sandra suggested. "Is there somewhere we can walk to from here? It's a really nice afternoon."

"Yeah, there's a diner a couple of blocks from here," he said.

"YES!" Lucy jumped up and down, excited. "It's great, Sandra, you'll love it. The waitresses wear roller skates!"

"Oh, it's a fifties diner?" Sandra asked.

Kody nodded. "Yeah, would that be okay?"

Sandra smiled. "Perfect."

"Go get changed and wash up, Lucy, and

then we'll go for a walk." Kody watched as Lucy happily pranced down the hall to do that.

"She seems happy," Sandra said.

"She loves the fifties diner. You just made her night."

"Good."

"And you'll be okay eating that?"

She shrugged. "If I can get french fries, I should be. I had some Chinese food that Megan brought last night. It was great."

"Yes. I'm going to have to have a talk with Dr. Coombs."

"No, don't," Sandra said. "She's really sweet and I don't have many friends here. You have to work, and I don't want you to scare her off. If you did, I would have to kick your purple butt!"

"My dad has a purple butt?" Lucy asked, sneaking up behind them.

Kody laughed. "Not since high school. Now, why don't we go have some dinner at the diner?" Which, given the state of his unpreparedness for dinner in the first place and the disaster of not being able to focus on a chicken dinner, was what they should've done right from the very start.

The dinner at the diner was exactly what she needed. She'd forgotten how much she liked french fries. And Lucy really seemed to be enjoying herself. Truth be told, Sandra was too. She hadn't planned on eating fries in a diner. She'd been hoping to spend time with Kody and Lucy at their house, where they could talk about things without having to shout above The Big Bopper and Buddy Holly.

Still, it was fun.

And she couldn't remember the last time she'd had so much fun.

Lucy was an absolute delight and Sandra found herself longing for something more, which she couldn't have. She and Kody had made a promise that they didn't have to commit to one another.

She wasn't sure about opening her heart again because of Alex, and he was still grieving his late wife, but now there was a part of her that wished she hadn't made that promise. She wished that she could be hopeful for something more.

After their dinner, they wandered just a bit beyond the fifties diner and found a soft-serve ice-cream shack, which literally looked like a dirty old shack on the outside, except for the side of the building, which had been transformed by a mural artist, who had painted a beautiful sunrise. Just like the sunrises that she often experienced in the morning from her kitchen.

Inside the shack was an immaculate soft-serve ice-cream place that served up sugary twists of cool, soft ice cream. They all got a small cone and slowly walked back to Kody's house, Lucy skipping ahead of them. They decided to take a walk to the local playground, so that Lucy could burn off some steam on the swings and the slides.

It was like something out of a dream.

It was something she'd always imagined in her deepest, most sacred dreams. It was something that she'd never thought would happen, especially when her doctor in San Diego had told her she wouldn't get pregnant.

She could get used to a Sunday like this more often.

Don't get too attached.

Her anxiety reminded her that the last time she'd got too attached that man had broken her heart.

"Why do you want a divorce? I thought we were happy?" she demanded.

"We were, but then I got stressed, Sandra. All the fertility treatments... There was no spontaneity to our sex life. And you turned into a totally different person."

"It was the hormones, Alex. You know that. You're a doctor!"

"I'm sorry, Sandra. Adoption is not for me and I'm not even sure I want kids."

Her world dropped out beneath her.

"You don't want kids? You told me you did when we got married."

"I don't know. But I know I don't want to adopt. You can't have children and you want a family, and I'm not sure I can support your decision. I'm not sure I'm the right man for you after all."

"Hey, you okay?" Kody asked, waving a hand in front of her face.

"What?"

"You zoned out there and seemed so sad," he said.

"Just thinking about something. Something that is not important."

"Are you sure?"

"Yeah. Pretty sure."

They had come to the park and Lucy was running straight for the activity equipment while Sandra and Kody found a park bench. She'd finished her ice cream off and just enjoyed a nice summer evening in a park, listening to the cottonwood leaves rustling in the evening wind.

"It's so beautiful here," she said.

"Austin is a beautiful city. Although your stretch of land just outside the city is beautiful too. I'd rather live out there than in the city limits."

"Maybe one day you will." She smiled at him. "Maybe one day you'll get your pilot's license and you'll need a big piece of property for a landing strip."

"If I can afford that after I get my pilot's license. Do you know how expensive flying lessons are?"

"Yes, but pilots make a lot of money."

"Commercial pilots, but I don't think that air-ambulance pilots do. Not around here when there are a lot of hospitals for people to get to. Maybe up north, but, even then, there's the high cost of living."

"So you've thought about this?" she asked.

"Of course. Jenny and I were making plans to do just that, until she got pregnant. Besides, I've lived in Texas for so long now I don't even think I'd be able to handle negative forty and days of endless night. And my sister is here and Jenny's parents and..."

"And?" she asked.

"You."

She felt the heat bloom in her cheeks. "I don't want to be a reason to hold you back from your dreams."

"You're not. We all have to grow up sometime and I'm a paramedic. I love my job. I love being the first one on the scene and helping where I can. I love thinking two steps ahead so that I can get the patient to the hospital alive, so that you doctors have a better chance of saving that patient. I'm the first one there and I'm their best shot. I like that. I like being able to be a part of saving lives."

"And as one of those doctors, we do appreciate those who do a good job, like you and your sister. You make our jobs easier."

He grinned at her. "That's the first time a doctor has ever thanked me."

"Really?"

He nodded. "I guess we don't really get a chance to socialize often with doctors."

She didn't say anything more.

"Daddy! Look, it's Grandma and Grandpa."

Kody's spine stiffened and Sandra saw the older couple who she'd first seen the day after the mudslide, walking across the park toward them.

"Your in-laws are here?"

"Yes," Kody said, and she could hear the stress in his voice.

"Go talk to them."

"Yeah, okay, I'll be back in a moment. I'm not… I'm not ready for them to meet you."

She understood what he meant, but still it stung like a slap. He might not be ready to introduce her, but what about when the baby came? When he had an infant in tow when he dropped Lucy off to see them? His in-laws had a right to know.

So she watched from a distance, as she had before. His in-laws briefly glanced at her, but nothing more, and she felt as if she was an outsider again, when for one brief moment she'd felt as if she were a part of Kody's little family.

It was a sharp reminder of why she had put walls up.

Why she didn't get involved.

Rejection, even when unintentional, still hurt.

CHAPTER EIGHT

KODY WAS BUSY with work.

At least that was what he told her after their nice time in the park had been cut short when Jenny's parents showed up. Not that Sandra blamed them in the slightest. They didn't know, but since that chance encounter Kody had pulled back and kept his distance.

And Sandra had given him the space he needed.

It had been a couple of weeks and she was bored out of her gourd. Megan came by every once in a while to tell her the progress of what was going on with her trauma department or some other kind of gossip that Sandra really didn't care about, but it was a distraction from the boredom.

At least today she was supposed to see Kody. She was going to meet him at the hospital for her OB/GYN appointment. It had been a couple of weeks since Dr. Ohe first confirmed that she was pregnant, and Sandra was anxious about today. She was worried that when she went there today Dr. Ohe wouldn't be able to find a heartbeat or that the pregnancy was gone.

You haven't had cramps. You haven't had spotting.

She would be ten weeks. Six weeks was the longest she'd ever carried a baby so twelve seemed too good to be true.

She parked her car in the employee lot and walked to the main entrance. She was early and she needed time to think, and a nice, casual stroll from the employee lot to the main entrance was exactly what she needed to clear her head and to think about everything.

Although she couldn't really begin to wrap her mind around much. It was as if her brain had turned to mush or something.

All she knew was she was going stir-crazy and she had to do something. She wasn't crafty, so taking up a crafty type of hobby wasn't her thing.

There's the DNA test.

She had told Kody that she was going to get her DNA tested and find out what hereditary diseases she might be at risk for, but she hadn't done that yet. Nor had she applied to the courts to see about obtaining information about her biological parents. She'd always put it off—maybe it was time to pursue that.

Even if she was terrified about the prospect.

If she didn't apply to have her adoption records opened, she was at least going to get her DNA tested and she was positive that Jocelyn could help her with that by administering the blood test.

When she got up to the maternity floor, she didn't see Kody anywhere.

"Did Mr. Davis come by?" Sandra asked the receptionist.

"No. I'm sorry, Dr. Fraser."

"Thanks." Sandra tried to hide her disappointment, but really it wasn't a surprise to her. After they'd run into Jenny's parents in the park, something had changed with Kody

174 PREGNANT WITH THE PARAMEDIC'S BABY

and she'd been worried that this was going to happen.

This is why you have walls. This is why you have boundaries.

"Dr. Fraser? Dr. Ohe will see you now."

Sandra nodded and followed the nurse into the exam rooms. The nurse took her BP, did a finger stick to test for her glucose levels and gave her a cup with an orange lid so that she could give them a urine specimen.

After Sandra did all of that and left the specimen in the washroom, she headed back to her exam room and waited for Jocelyn to come in.

"Well, Sandra, I have good news," Jocelyn said as she entered the room. "You're still showing consistent HCG levels in your urine. This is a good sign."

"Good," Sandra whispered.

"Do you want to wait for Mr. Davis?" Jocelyn asked.

Sandra glanced at the clock on the wall. He knew what time her appointment was, and it was obvious that he wasn't coming.

"No, he's probably held up at an emergency or something."

Jocelyn nodded. "Have you thought about getting a DNA test done? I know you've mentioned that to me before."

"I would like one done. I'm hoping you can do the blood work?"

"Of course." Jocelyn set down her tablet, which contained Sandra's file, and prepared stuff to draw some blood. "I'll also take a couple of vials for my normal tests."

"Good. Let's get it over and done with," Sandra said, rolling up her sleeve.

Jocelyn wiped her arm with an alcohol swab. "Little prick. There. I like doing some tests on doctors because I don't have to explain much."

Sandra smiled.

Jocelyn finished her blood draw, added labels to the vials and called for a nurse, who came and took the blood work away and then off to Pathology.

"So what now?" Sandra asked.

"We'll check for a heartbeat on the Doppler. If I don't pick one up, it doesn't mean that there isn't one there. It just means it's too early for the Doppler to pick it up, but we'll do an ultrasound anyway, to check that everything is where it should be."

Sandra nodded. "That would be great. I'm having a hard time believing that it's still there and viable."

"You feeling better?"

"Sort of. Kody made me this tea that seems to be helping. He gave me the recipe and I've been drinking it faithfully." Sandra pulled up the recipe on her phone and Jocelyn examined it.

"Ah, yes, that's similar to one my *halmoni* would make for us when we were sick. Usually after the long flight back to Seoul from Boston. I got the worst motion sickness when I was a kid."

"Kody said it worked well for him as a kid too, and, though I was skeptical, I have to admit it is working."

"Well, it's perfectly safe, so if it's working, then keep using it." Jocelyn pulled off her gloves and disposed of them. "Now, lie back and we'll see if we can find a heartbeat. I also want to chat with you about setting up a glucose fasting test at sixteen weeks and an amniocentesis."

"You're getting too far ahead for me, Jocelyn."

"You're a trauma surgeon—I thought you liked to think ahead?" Jocelyn teased as she lifted Sandra's shirt.

"Well, this is all overwhelming and I don't want to get too far ahead of myself."

"Understandable." Jocelyn flicked on the Doppler. It made a static sound as Jocelyn ran the wand over her belly.

Sandra closed her eyes and tried not to let her emotions get the best of her as they waited, listening for a sound.

She's not going to find any sound. There's no heartbeat. Why did you think this was going to work?

And just as those self-destructive thoughts were running through her mind she heard it. A sound…a fast noise that was so different that it had her heart pounding and her blood rushing through her body.

It was the sound of something alive inside her.

Her baby.

"There's the heartbeat. Nice and strong." Jocelyn smiled at her, her dark eyes warm. "Congratulations."

Sandra was fighting back the tears, but she couldn't stop them from slipping down her cheeks, down the sides of her face and into her ears because she was lying on her back. The baby was there. There was a baby, alive, inside of her.

It was strong and it was still there. Her baby.

"We'll do an ultrasound so I can check to make sure that everything is okay."

Sandra nodded her head in agreement, because she couldn't find the words to say. She was so moved with emotion, but she was sad that Kody was missing this. That Kody wasn't here to hear their baby's heartbeat.

Even if it had been awkward after Jenny's

parents saw them in the park, this wasn't like him. He wanted this baby.

He'd told her that.

It's his loss.

And then another part of her worried that this might be the only time that she would get to hear the heartbeat, because, at ten weeks, she was not out of the danger zone yet. Sandra knew that she wouldn't feel completely safe about this pregnancy until she was past the point for when a baby could survive out of utero.

She had to get to twenty-five weeks minimum. She just had to.

"Are you okay?" Jocelyn asked.

"Just worrying."

"It's understandable." She turned on the monitor and it didn't take her long to find the baby. "See, everything looks good. The baby has a strong heartbeat and there's a little arm. The baby is quite active. That's a good sign. Your placenta is in a good spot. So far, so good, Sandra. I still want you to take it easy. I still don't want you working."

"It's driving me crazy not working. I hope that you know that."

"Did you have any research you wanted to get done?" Jocelyn asked.

"What do you mean?"

Jocelyn shrugged. "Some kind of new innovation that you've always wanted to research, but just couldn't because you were a trauma surgeon and always on the go?"

"Yes. I suppose I had a couple of ideas tucked away for when I had time to pursue it."

"Now's the time," Jocelyn said, wiping up her belly. "You may be on light duty, but I know that the chief wouldn't mind if you used your sabbatical to actually pursue something good for the hospital. Rolling Creek has an extensive library and a research lab. All you have to do is make a proposal to the board of directors."

"When is the next board meeting?" Sandra asked, intrigued.

"In a month. That's plenty of time to get a project up and running."

Sandra felt excited. It was perfect. It was

exactly the thing she needed to stop her from going stir-crazy and worrying about whether or not Kody was all in.

This was something she could finally devote time to, and maybe even get a grant from the hospital board of directors to help fund it.

"Here's a picture to show Kody and it's a keepsake for you." Jocelyn slipped the ultrasound image into an envelope. "I want to see you in a month."

"A month?" Sandra asked, shocked and nervous.

"Yep, unless there's spotting or cramping or anything that freaks you out. Right now, you're doing well. Rest, study and get that proposal ready."

"Thanks, Jocelyn."

Jocelyn smiled at her and left the exam room. Sandra slipped the envelope into her purse. She was so excited to go home, fire up her computer and go through her old files. She had a purpose again. She may not be in the operating room like she wanted to be or out on the trauma floor saving lives, but this would at least keep her sane.

Keep her connected to the job she loved.
And keep her mind off Kody.

Sandra was so lost in her thoughts that she didn't hear her name being called across the lobby. Finally she clued into the fact that Dr. Fraser was her and that she was being paged.

She turned around to see Kody's sister, Sally Davis, running toward her. She was in her paramedic uniform and she looked frightened.

Sandra's stomach did a flip and her heart sank.

Oh, God.

"Sally?" Sandra rushed over to her. "What's happened?"

"Kody's rig was in an accident. Robbie is pretty hurt and is in surgery. Kody has a concussion and a couple of broken ribs. He was on his way to the appointment. Please know he didn't ditch you."

Sandra was shocked. "So you know."

Sally blushed. "I do. He told me. He really wanted to be there."

"I believe you."

Sally sighed, relieved. "Good."

"What about Lucy?" Sandra asked.

"Jenny's parents took Lucy to Disneyland for a small holiday. They left yesterday." Sally worried her bottom lip. "The accident the rig was in was part of a huge chain on the highway—a transport truck flipped and there are more injured. I have to get back out there, but they won't discharge him unless he has somewhere to go."

"I can take him back to my place and watch him. You go."

Sally nodded. "Thank you, Sandra. I know this is awkward for you…"

"Go," Sandra insisted. "I'll watch him for the next twenty-four hours and make sure he doesn't exacerbate his concussion."

Sally nodded again and ran back toward the ambulance bay. There would be more injured coming in and if Kody was stable enough to be discharged, he had to make room for the other injured that would be brought in soon.

Sandra made her way down to the trauma department and found out where Kody was being kept. She pulled back the curtain and he was lying there, his head stitched and his chest bandaged, to hold the ribs in place.

He looked bruised and broken. And it made her so upset to see him like that. And the realization hit her that she could've lost him. Her baby would've lost its father, and she tried to hold back the tears that were threatening to come.

"So, I guess I know why you missed the appointment."

He smiled weakly at her; he was obviously drugged up. "How's Robbie?"

"I don't know. I know he's in surgery."

"He was thrown, you see. We were stopped helping a patient and a transport truck rammed into the back of the rig. I wasn't in the rig, but Robbie was."

Sandra's stomach did a flip-flop. "Oh, my God. You could've been killed."

"Where's Sally? She's supposed to take me home, but I told her I'm not leaving until I know that Robbie is okay."

"Sally had to go back to work. There're more injured. As soon as I find a doctor, I'm going to take you back to my place. You have to be watched for the next couple of days to make sure you don't have a concussion and you don't injure yourself further. You have broken ribs, my friend."

Kody chuckled and closed his eyes.

"He's pretty high," Dr. Murdoch said, coming in. "Dr. Fraser, it's good to see you. How are things?"

"Good. Kody's sister, Sally, is still on duty, so I'm going to take Kody home and I can keep an eye on him."

Burt nodded. "Good. So I don't have to explain concussion protocols to you?"

"No. Could you have a couple of orderlies get him up and in a wheelchair? I'll drive my car around to the emergency entrance."

"I can certainly do that for you, Dr. Fraser."

"Thanks, Burt. Oh, and how is Kody's partner, Robbie?"

Burt frowned. "It's not looking good. He has severe internal injuries. His Glasgow coma scale on arrival was three."

Sandra's heart sank. That was not a good prognosis. "Can you keep me informed? Kody's worried about him."

"I can. Take him home and make sure he gets rest and I'll let the fire station know that he's off work until those ribs heal, at least. If he has a concussion, he'll be off longer."

"Thanks, Burt."

Dr. Murdoch handed her the discharge papers and Kody roused again.

"Sandra! What're you doing here?"

"Oh. Boy. You're high, all right. I'm going to take you home. A couple of orderlies are going to help you up and I'm going to meet you out front with my car."

"Cool."

Sandra tried not to laugh and left the emergency room. She waved to a few people who waved to her, but everyone was busy tending to those who had been brought in from the accident and getting ready for those who were still incoming.

It took Sandra twenty minutes to drive from the employee parking lot to the emergency department because of a traffic jam and a minor fender bender on the thoroughfare. When she got down to the emergency department doors, an orderly was sitting with Kody, who was laughing to himself in a wheelchair.

Sandra parked her SUV and got out, opening the passenger-side door.

"It hurst when I laugh," Kody said brightly.

"It 'hurst'? You mean it hurts, don't you?"

Kody grinned and winked. "Right, I think my ribs are broken, baby."

Sandra rolled her eyes. "Come on, Captain Obvious, into the car."

Once Sandra had Kody secure, the orderly left and Sandra climbed back into the driver side. She had Kody's prescription for pain meds that she'd call in and have delivered, but first she had to stop at his house and get him a change of clothes and make sure everything was locked up there.

Kody didn't really say much. He just leaned against the seat and dozed on and off. She found his key in his jacket pocket and ran inside his house to pack him an overnight bag. His room was surprisingly neat, so she found everything no problem.

When she opened his shirt drawer, she found a picture, in a frame. It was Jenny. A picture of a young woman, but it was Jenny nonetheless.

She was pretty, but it wasn't the first time she'd seen a picture of Lucy's mother. They were all over the house, but Sandra couldn't help but wonder why this picture was hidden away in Kody's shirt drawer. And as she looked around the room, there was no other sign of Jenny anywhere else.

Which made her feel guilty. As if she was intruding.

Focus. You don't want him to wake up and get out of the SUV, do you?

Sandra finished her packing and then locked up his house, making sure everything was secure. When she came back to the SUV, Kody was still snoozing away.

Great. He's drooling on his shirt.

And that made her laugh to herself.

By the time they got to her house he was waking up again and appeared to be more lucid.

"Where am I?" he asked groggily.

"At my place."

"Sandra, when did you get here?"

"Sally is still working, and you need someone to watch you. You might have a concussion and you definitely have some broken ribs."

Kody moaned. "Yeah. I can feel that."

"Robbie is in surgery still, but Dr. Murdoch said that he'd keep me posted."

Kody groaned. "Oh, God. I hope… We switched places and that should've been me in the rig."

"But it wasn't. Robbie is in good hands. Come on, I have actually set up a guest bed this time, so you have a place to sleep, instead of on my couch."

Kody nodded and she helped him out of her SUV and up the steps into her home. She had his bag slung over her shoulder and her purse on the other shoulder.

"You packed me a bag?"

"You need clothes. You're still in your uniform. Don't worry, I didn't find that stack of naughty magazines." She winked and he winced.

"Don't make me laugh. It hurts."

"Sorry." She led him to her guest bedroom. It held a queen-size bed and she'd just bought a new duvet and sheet set for it. There hadn't been much else to do the last couple of weeks that she'd been off.

She got him settled on the bed and then started unbuttoning his uniform. Her hands were trembling as she did that, because the last time she'd undressed him, they'd made this baby together.

"You don't have to do that. I can," he said.

"You need to not move around so much. Let me help."

He nodded, but he wouldn't look her in the eyes. There was an undercurrent of something there and her pulse began to race.

"Okay, I think you can manage the rest." She set his duffel bag on the bed next to him.

He nodded. "Thanks."

"No problem. You would and have done the same for me. This room also has a private bathroom that's stocked. If you need anything, just holler."

"Thanks, Sandra. I will."

She slipped out of the room and shut the door.

This was the right thing to do, but this was also going to be tough.

They couldn't be together.

They both had commitment issues. It was just, when she was around him, all those fears seemed to melt away and what she wanted was something more from him.

She wanted to be with him.

And that thought scared her.

Kody got out of his uniform and went into the bathroom. His head was pounding and all the natural light pouring in through the skylight just made his headache worse. He had some stitches along the hairline—superficial cuts, most likely—and he knew he was going to get a black eye. He could feel that.

His ribs hurt bad and were turning all sorts of shades of purple and blue. A slight move made everything hurt.

Still, he'd fared better than Robbie.

Robbie was in surgery. Robbie, who had

just proposed to his nurse girlfriend last week, was in surgery, fighting for his life.

And it was all his fault for wanting to switch spots on the rig.

Kody sighed. If something happened to Robbie, he doubted he could ever forgive himself.

It wasn't your fault. You couldn't have known.

Still, he could've paid better attention to what was happening out on the road, but he'd been so preoccupied with the fact that he'd been missing Sandra's OB/GYN appointment. He'd wanted to be there. Everything had been so awkward after running into Ted and Myrtle. He didn't want Sandra to think he was ducking out, because he wasn't.

That night in the park, when Jenny's parents had seemed to materialize from nowhere, it had reminded him that he wasn't supposed to be at a park with Lucy and another woman. It had made him feel horribly guilty.

Myrtle had noticed Sandra too and asked if she was his girlfriend and he'd denied it.

He'd told her that Sandra was new to Austin and worked at the hospital, but hadn't mentioned that she was a surgeon, or that she was carrying his baby.

He couldn't tell them.

It would be a betrayal. He was already feeling bad about taking down the picture he had of Jenny in his room and putting it away.

Then a horrible thought crept into his mind. What if Sandra had seen the picture in his drawer? What would she think of him?

He winced in pain and headed back to bed. If he didn't need to be on a concussion watch, he wouldn't be here. He wouldn't have let her take him here. He just would've gone home and suffered in silence, which was what he preferred to do.

Not only was he feeling bad about Jenny's parents and Robbie, but he was feeling awful about missing Sandra's appointment. It was his baby too and he wanted his child and he was really regretting not being there today for the checkup.

Kody climbed back into bed, tried to arrange the pillows the best he could and closed his eyes. He knew that he couldn't watch TV or read or do anything until they knew that he didn't have a concussion. All he could do was lie here.

And that was boring as heck.

There was a gentle knock on his door.

"Come in, Sandra."

She came in, holding a white paper bag and a glass of water. "I have your medications. I figure you might be feeling some pain."

"Yeah, just a touch." Kody winced.

She sat down on the edge of the bed and handed him the water glass, then pulled out a bottle of pain medication. "No ibuprofen for you—not until you're cleared of a concussion."

Kody took the pills and swallowed them down with the water. He leaned back against the pillows, wincing. He'd never broken his ribs before, and he wasn't sure that he wanted to again. Everything hurt in the upper part of his body, his shoulders, his back, his sides. It was like a thousand knives stabbing him.

"You have to be careful. They're hairline fractures, but, still, you don't want to make a hairline fracture something more and risk injuring your soft tissue or your lungs," Sandra warned.

"How long am I off work?" he muttered.

"Six weeks for fractured ribs."

"What?" Kody gasped, and then it hurt to take that deep breath.

"Calm down." She handed him another pill. "It's a muscle relaxant. It should help."

"I can't live here for six weeks. Lucy's only gone for one."

"You're going to need help. You can't do any heavy lifting, but you should be able to mostly manage in about a week. And hopefully you don't have a concussion, because that will just prolong everything."

Six weeks. He was going to be out of work for six weeks. And if Robbie survived, he would be out even longer.

He wasn't supposed to be the injured one; he was supposed to be out there helping others and doing his job. He was supposed to be saving lives.

"I know you're frustrated. I get it."

"You seem calmer than usual, though,"

Kody remarked. "I take it the appointment went well."

"It did." She smiled. "And now I understand why you didn't make it."

"Yeah. I'm sorry."

"No apologies. I get it."

"I'm glad everything went well," he said, and he truly meant it.

Sandra pulled out a picture, handing it to him. "Here's your copy. Our baby."

His heart warmed as he stared at the blurry, grainy picture of a little alien-looking creature floating around in what looked like outer space. He always thought that was funny. He always thought it was cute to see and this was no exception.

He smiled. "I'm glad."

"I go and see Jocelyn again in a month. She also took blood work to test my DNA and see if I have any genetic worries."

"I thought you did that already?" he asked.

"I put it off, but it's done now."

"I'm glad you got it done." He gingerly set the picture on the nightstand, so that he could see it. "What else did she say?"

"She came up with an idea to keep me active. I'm not much of a crafty-type person and there's only so much television I can watch."

"Oh? And what is this great idea to keep you busy and not hurt yourself?"

"I'm putting together a proposal for one of my old research ideas. The proposal is due in a month and if the board of directors approves, I'll get grant money and time in the research labs at the hospital. So, I'll be at work, but not doing anything that would endanger me or the baby."

"That's great! So what're you going to work on?"

"I don't know. I haven't had a chance to go through my files and find something yet. Someone got in an accident."

"I didn't do it on purpose!"

She smiled. "I know. I just like teasing you. You're fun to tease when you can't fight back."

"Ha. Ha." He yawned; the medicine was starting to take effect. Muscle relaxers and a painkiller—he was feeling very sedated.

"I think you need sleep," Sandra whispered.

She got up and pulled the duvet up around him. "Try and rest. We'll see how you fare and whether you need to go back to the hospital to get a CT for a concussion."

"Right," he murmured. "If you hear anything about Robbie…"

"I'll let you know." She walked to the door and closed it.

Even though he didn't want to be here and didn't want to burden Sandra, when all was said and done, he was glad she'd taken him in. He would have had nowhere else to go. Sally was working and busy with her own life.

And he didn't want to disrupt Lucy's trip to Disneyland with her grandparents. So he was glad that Sandra had offered to take him in. Even if it was for just a week.

He was glad he could count on her friendship.

Even if he wanted more than friendship.

So much more.

CHAPTER NINE

KODY HEARD THE phone ringing, in what he assumed was the middle of the night. It made his head pound and the room was dark. There was no clock in the guest room, and he'd forgotten to charge his phone.

He really was out of it. When he tried to move, it was painful, and he hoped that Sandra would come and tell him the news. Although, news during the night was never a good sign.

Please don't let Robbie die.

And he felt responsible for Robbie because he was supposed to be in the back of the rig. It should have been him and he felt guilty that it wasn't.

There was a knock at the door.

"Come in," he called out.

Sandra slipped in. "That was the hospital."

"Tell me something good."

"Robbie's stable and in the ICU. He survived the surgery. They're not sure if he'll walk again, though. I'm sorry, Kody."

Kody sighed.

Oh, God.

Robbie was so young and active. It wasn't fair.

When was life fair?

"If I hadn't switched spots with him…"

"You could've been killed. You don't know how your body would've taken it compared to his." She came and sat down on the bed next to him, putting her hand on his shoulder. It was comforting. "And that would leave Lucy without any parents and our baby without his or her father. It's not your fault, you didn't know. You couldn't have known."

"You're right."

"Well, he's in good hands and he survived the surgery. They didn't think that he would." Sandra was trying to comfort him. He appreciated it, but it wasn't helping.

"That's good at least."

"Well, I should get back to bed. It's midnight."

"I was wondering what time it was, but you don't have to leave. I'm wide awake—why don't you stay awhile?"

"You might be wide awake, but I'm exhausted."

"Just stay."

Sandra sighed. "Fine, but I'm getting under the covers and if I fall asleep don't wake me up."

"Deal." He shifted over slightly so that she had room. She placed her phone on the other nightstand on her side and curled up on her side, away from him.

He recalled the feeling of her behind against him when he'd spooned her in the cabin. How he wished he could spoon her now. How he wanted to curl up next to her and hold her in his arms, but he could barely move, and he didn't want to do further damage to his ribs. It was bad enough that he was going to be missing out on six weeks of work.

Robbie's going to miss a lot more.

Kody shook that thought from his head.

He didn't want to think about that possibility. Robbie was alive and he'd help his friend any way he could. Right now, he wanted to sleep, even if he couldn't.

"So I thought you would've turned this room into a nursery?" he asked.

Sandra yawned. "There're two more bedrooms. One is closer to my room—that will be the nursery. The other room is on the opposite side of the house and it's not finished yet."

"Well, don't be thinking of doing any major renovation."

"You really want to talk about home renovating at midnight?" she asked, her tone slightly surly.

"I do. It keeps my mind off other things."

"Like what?" she asked, her voice muffled into her pillow.

"I was thinking about how we fell asleep in the cabin. How nice it felt to have your bottom pressed against me." He was teasing her, there was no way he could do anything about it right now, but he couldn't help but think about her since she was sharing his bed.

He thought about that night a lot.

Sandra rolled over and glared at him in the darkness. He could see the glint in her eyes from the moonlight streaming in through the wooden blinds. "Why are we talking about this right now?"

"Hey, you got some good teases in earlier. I'm sure I was quite funny on painkillers."

"You were and I got it on video."

His blood ran cold. "What?"

"You know how when people are high after dental surgery or after receiving really strong pain meds after their broken bones are set?"

"You did not."

She chuckled wickedly. "You were sitting in a wheelchair laughing and laughing, telling me how much you were in pain. It was hilarious. And then you drooled all over your shirt on the ride back to my place."

"You did not video me."

"No," she finally admitted. "But I should next time. It might be good for blackmail."

"You're slightly evil, Dr. Fraser."

"So I've been told. Now go to sleep."

"You have to get used to this," he persisted.

"What?"

"People keeping you up. Kids keeping you up. I'm just training you for the inevitable."

"If you weren't injured, I would seriously slug you," she muttered.

Kody chuckled softly, but it hurt too much. "Good night, Sandra."

"Night," she murmured, and it wasn't long before he heard gentle snoring. He tried to relax against the pillows, but he couldn't sleep. His brain was just running. Usually, when he couldn't shut his mind down, he went and did some physical activity. Lifted weights, did some cardio, but all of that was out of the question.

He slowly slipped out of bed and found the charger to his phone. He plugged it in and waited for the screen to turn on. He was worried that he might've missed a call from Lucy or a text message, but he hadn't.

Myrtle and Ted knew that he was working long hours this week. Or he was supposed to be. He checked his social-media feeds and saw pictures of Lucy dressed as her favorite princess and having a great time.

He was envious of their vacation.

He wished he could be there, but work had to come first. It was how he provided for her and how he would have to help provide for the new baby.

He set his phone back down and climbed back into bed next to Sandra, trying not to disturb her. He wished he could roll on his side to sleep—that was usually how he slept. He never slept on his back and that was probably why he was having a hard time shutting his mind down to get rest.

You know that's not the reason.

Try as he might, he knew the real reason that he couldn't sleep was the fact he was in bed with Sandra and there wasn't a damn thing he could do about it, even if he wanted to.

Well, he wanted to physically, but he wasn't going to hurt her. He wasn't going to do anything to hurt her the way she'd been hurt in the past and unless he could give his whole heart to her, then he couldn't give anything of himself to her.

It wasn't fair to her.

You gave a piece of yourself. She's carrying your child.

His head was starting to hurt, and he knew that he needed to get some rest. He seriously doubted he had a concussion, but there was no point in tempting fate. He closed his eyes and tried to drift off to sleep.

Even if the rest of him was wide awake.

Sandra woke the next morning, startled at her location and the fact she was sharing a bed with Kody. She'd forgotten that she'd come in last night to give Kody an update on Robbie and that Kody had begged her to stay. She'd only been intending to stay for a little while. She hadn't planned on spending the entire night.

She usually tossed and turned in her sleep and she was worried that she'd somehow hurt Kody, but she gently rolled over and saw that he was fine. He was on his back, his mouth wide open and catching flies.

And she couldn't help but laugh quietly to herself.

She took this as a good opportunity to slip

out of bed and get started on her research proposal, which was what she had been excited to start when Jocelyn had first suggested it, before the accident happened.

She got dressed in her room and then quietly made her way out into her living room. She had her tea all made and some dry toast, the sun was coming up and it was quiet. It was the perfect time to go through her old notes and see what she could find.

When she was a resident and learning under her attending, when she first decided to become a trauma surgeon, she was really interested in the way that army surgeons set up portable emergency rooms in the harshest environments. A hospital was a great place to practice emergency medicine, but she always felt that doctors in this field didn't get the real hands-on experience that surgeons in the armed forces did.

It was a pipe dream of hers to start a course at the hospital that would teach residents the importance of fieldwork medicine. It was important to also extend this knowledge for the paramedics and other first responders.

Rolling Creek didn't have a simulation lab. They ran simulations, but they didn't have the state-of-the-art lab that her hospital in San Diego had had. And that was a shame, since Rolling Creek was a great hospital in a burgeoning city.

And then Sandra knew what she wanted to work on.

She wanted to develop a course to teach residents, surgeons and first responders about large-scale disasters and how to practice medicine in less than ideal situations.

Her brain lit up and she began typing up her proposal as fast as her fingers would let her. It was the first time in a long time that she'd felt so energized and excited.

"Sandra?" Kody called her name and she glanced over her shoulder to see him walking into the living room. He was holding his side, but he was dressed.

"Oh, sorry. Did I wake you?"

"No, it's almost noon. I'm sorry that I slept in."

"It's almost noon?" She checked the time

on her computer, and he was right. She'd been working for four hours nonstop.

"What're you doing?" he asked and came and sat down on the couch.

"Well, Jocelyn suggested that I work on a proposal for a research grant. That way I can still work and keep my mind focused on the medicine, but not be risking my health or the baby's health by being on my feet all day on the trauma floor."

"I think you told me this, but I really can't remember. It seems familiar." He yawned.

She laughed. "You weren't remembering much yesterday, my friend."

"So, what's your proposal about?" he asked.

"A new course and a proposal for an upgraded simulation lab. I want to be able to teach the first responders as well as the doctors how to set up a mobile emergency room. One that can be used in large-scale disasters, especially in times when it isn't feasible to get the patients to the hospital, but time is of the essence to save their life."

"That sounds great and it sounds like something I would love to take."

She smiled, pleased that Kody was into it. "How did you sleep last night?"

"Terribly. I couldn't get comfortable. I sleep on my side and not my back."

"I'm the opposite. I sleep on my stomach and back, not my side, but I can't sleep on my back. When I do, I feel this pressure, probably from the baby."

"Then we're both a bit skunked, aren't we?" he teased.

"How is your head?"

"Good. Other than the stitches hurting, I don't think that I have a concussion."

"Well, that's lucky." She saved her work. "I'll get you something to eat. You just stay there."

The moment she'd been told that it was noon, her stomach had growled. She knew it was better to eat small meals more frequently when you were pregnant, but she had been completely absorbed in her work and excited for it.

She made up a couple of sandwiches and brought them out for Kody on a tray with some sweet tea for him and his medications.

"Thanks," he said, wincing and setting down his phone. "That was Sally. Robbie is doing well and his leg was moving. So hopefully no paralysis. I told her my head was as fine as it could be."

"I'm sure she had something interesting to say when you told her that."

Kody chuckled. "Yeah, Sweet Pea always did have a scathing retort or two."

"She cares about you a lot, though, scathing retorts aside. You're lucky."

He nodded. "I know and I care about her too. And you."

His admission caught her off guard. "What?"

"I care about you, Sandra. How could I not? You're carrying my baby."

"You've been avoiding me since that moment in the park with your in-laws."

He sighed. "I know. I was feeling guilty."

"For what?"

"I don't know."

It was a lie. Sandra could see right through that. She was good at reading people working in the emergency room, but she wasn't going to push him. She just hoped in time that he would tell his in-laws about their baby, because she hoped that Kody would be in her baby's life.

"I want to thank you again for the picture of the baby," he said. "I'm sorry I wasn't there."

"There was an accident. I understand."

"I know, but I still wanted to be there."

"We should tell people now. Your daughter and your in-laws should be the next to know...since Sally already knows."

"Right. Yeah, we should."

He's lying again.

And that made her hurt.

What did you expect?

And she didn't know how to answer that. She didn't know what to expect.

The week went by smoothly.

Kody was healing nicely and didn't have a concussion. By day three he was moving around easily, and Sandra had checked his ribs. There was a lot of bruising, but for the most part he was doing well.

Sandra continued to work on her grant proposal and Kody provided excellent insight on his time as a paramedic, which helped enormously.

It was nice living with him. It was nice to talk to someone in the morning and have meals with him. It was nice to sit out on her porch with sweet tea and watch the sunrise or sunset.

It was nice knowing that she wasn't alone. And she realized that when she'd been married to Alex, even though they'd been sleeping in the same bed and living together, she'd felt alone. Being here with Kody during this week he'd stayed with her was completely different than anything she'd ever experienced before.

It made her dread the end of the week, when he would have to return to his place because his daughter would be coming home.

Sandra wished things were different between the two of them and she wished Lucy and Kody could come and live with her and the new baby, but that was just a fantasy, and Sandra knew it was also all the hormones that were making her feel like this.

Which was so out of character for her.

It would be best when Kody went home so that she could get back to some semblance of normality.

At the end of the week Sally was coming to pick him up and take him home because Lucy was returning from her trip with her grandparents.

She found him packing his bag and she was sad watching him pack up to leave, but she understood. This was not his home.

"You got everything?" she asked, hoping that her voice remained steady and didn't betray her actual feelings.

"I think so." He picked up the sonogram of their baby. "Almost forgot this."

"Are you going to tell Lucy about the baby?"

"No. Not yet."

"Why?" She tried to hide her disappointment that he didn't seem to want anyone to know about the baby. He said he did, but she knew it was a lie. Why was he so ashamed of it? Was it her?

"We'll both tell Lucy, together," he said, smiling.

"Sure." Only she didn't really believe him. Even if he was happy about the baby, and she knew that he would love the baby, she knew that he wished it'd never happened. It was another child, with a woman who was not his wife.

It was just one more thing holding him back. She knew that.

And she felt guilty about it.

There was a knock at the door and Sandra let Kody finish packing so that she could let Sally in.

Sally smiled brightly at her. "Is he ready?"

"Almost. Can I get you something to drink?" Sandra asked.

"No. I'm good." Sally worried her bottom lip. "How are you feeling?"

"I'm feeling good. I'm just over eleven weeks now, but we haven't told Lucy. We wanted to wait until after the first trimester, given my history."

"That's understandable. Well, I'm glad you're feeling okay and I'm really very excited." Sally smiled at her. "I can't wait to meet him or her."

"Thanks. That means a lot." And it did, because Sandra had no one on her side that was excited for her. No family who cared.

She was alone.

"Hey, Sweet Pea. Is Lucy home yet?"

"Nope, their flight lands in an hour. So we can get you home and break the news about the accident to them then." Sally took Kody's bag and waved goodbye to her.

Sandra sighed. "Good luck with telling your in-laws about your accident. At least Lucy will be happy to have you home for a few more weeks."

"That she will. Thank you for taking care of me. I appreciate it." He leaned forward and kissed her on the top of her head. "I'll let you know how it goes and we'll talk soon about telling Lucy."

"Sure. Okay."

Kody left her house and Sandra stood at the door, watching Sally help him into her car and then drive away, leaving her alone again. The house was so quiet.

She hadn't realized how much she would miss him, but she knew it was for the best.

Was it?

Still, she was surprised by how much she missed him.

Kody was glad to be home. Sally got him all settled, and Kody just wandered around his tiny house in the city limits. When he looked outside his window, all he could see was a row of houses, cookie-cutter and similar to his. All lined up. There was no meadow, no foothills he could look at.

The backyards were tiny and there was no room to grow.

He was envious of Sandra's home. He'd enjoyed his week there. He'd enjoyed being with Sandra. Even though his house was smaller, coming back after a week with her, his house felt empty.

He really missed being with her. He missed their talks, he missed discussing her grant proposal and he missed being able to see her every day. To watch his child growing. Even though there was only a slight swell to her stomach, his baby was in there.

And he was excited for the day he could feel the baby move.

He was excited to tell Lucy about it.

As he was standing there a car pulled in the driveway behind his car.

"They're back, Sally!" Kody called out. His sister was puttering around in the kitchen.

Lucy came bounding up the steps. "Daddy!"

She made as if she wanted to jump up in his arms, but he took a step back and Lucy frowned, noticing his head was still bandaged. "Daddy, what's wrong? What happened?"

Myrtle and Ted came in and saw the bandage too.

"What happened?" Ted asked.

"My rig was in an accident." Kody took a seat on the couch and Lucy climbed up beside him, curling herself under his arm.

Myrtle gasped. "Oh, my gosh. Why didn't you tell us?"

"I was fine. I have some broken ribs and a head wound that's healed. But that's it. I'm off work for about six weeks."

"When did this happen?" Ted asked.

"The day after you left."

"You should have told us!" Myrtle chastised. "We would've come back."

"I was fine," Kody said. "I didn't want to ruin your vacation. I was well looked after. My doctor friend took care of me."

"Sandra?" Lucy piped up and instantly Kody regretted saying that his doctor friend had looked after him.

"Who is Sandra?" Myrtle asked.

"My doctor friend. She's new to Austin and, yes, she helped take care of me. Sally as well." He was hoping that was enough of an excuse, because he didn't want to have to explain Sandra to Myrtle and Ted right now.

"Well, we have something for you. Maybe on your six weeks off you can study for it," Ted said as he pulled out a flyer.

"What's this?" Kody asked.

"Flying lessons," Myrtle said. "We know that you and Jenny had plans and we know a lot of that was put on hold for so long, so we decided to start you off with some flying lessons. There's some bookwork you have to do, but you can start that now while you're off work."

Kody stared at the brochure. Stunned. He didn't know what to say; all he could feel was a gnawing sense of guilt.

Myrtle and Ted did so much for him, and how did he repay them? By moving on from their daughter.

"Thank you both." That was all he could say.

He couldn't tell them anything else, but he knew one thing.

He didn't deserve it.

He didn't deserve any of it.

CHAPTER TEN

Eight weeks later

SANDRA WALKED OUT of her second meeting with the board of directors since she had first submitted her proposal to them. She was feeling cautiously optimistic that the board was going to approve the work to add to their simulation lab and start the process of teaching residents and first responders the course she'd meticulously outlined.

The last eight weeks had flown by and even though she hadn't seen much of Kody, other than the occasional phone call to check how she was, she had really been able to hunker down and focus on her work.

She was hoping they would've told Lucy about the baby by now, but Lucy had been so distressed by Kody's accident they'd decided to wait. And then she didn't hear anything more.

She just hoped they decided to tell her soon because mostly everyone knew she was pregnant now. They could tell by the round swell of her belly. She had been slim to begin with and it was harder to hide the fact that she was pregnant, but the baby was still doing well. Still strong and, at nineteen weeks, her morning sickness had all but disappeared.

And she wanted Lucy to know, but she wasn't going to worry about it because there was nothing she could do.

Kody knew what was best for his daughter and she had to stop worrying about it.

The last thing she needed was stress and, after this board meeting, she was feeling like her old self again. She was feeling confident and ready to really get to work on the project. It might not be surgery, but it was still something she was passionate about.

"Sandra!"

Sandra turned to see Dr. Ohe coming toward her with an envelope.

"Jocelyn, it's good to see you. I didn't miss an appointment, did I?"

"No, no. I just knew that you were here today meeting the board of directors for a second time. How did it go?"

"Well, I think. I hope that it did."

"I'm sure that it did." Jocelyn took a deep breath and held out the envelope for Sandra to take. "Your DNA results."

Sandra's heart skipped a beat and she took the envelope from Jocelyn. "I don't know if I can open it. I got a letter from the state about my adoption record, but I haven't been able to open that one either."

"Well, this one won't have names, but you'll be able to see what is in your DNA. I had a glance. There's nothing too worrying that your baby might inherit."

Sandra let out a sigh of relief. "Well, that's at least something."

Jocelyn smiled. "Still, for your own sake you should read it and let me know if you have any questions."

"Thanks, Jocelyn." Sandra's hands trembled as she held the envelope.

Jocelyn left and Sandra wandered over to a quiet spot in the atrium of the hospital. She was staring at the envelope and didn't know what to make of it. She was glad that she had it, but she was terrified to open it.

You've been wondering about it for so long.

Only she couldn't do it. Not here. She jammed the envelope into her briefcase and glanced up in time to see Kody coming toward her. He was back in his paramedic's uniform. He looked happy to see her.

Don't be fooled. It's an act.

And she had to remind herself of that. Even if she wanted more, it was clear that he didn't, and she wasn't going to risk her heart again. No matter how much she wanted to.

"I thought that was you over there. What're you doing here, Sandra?" he asked.

"I could ask the same of you, but it's obvious you've been cleared to return to work."

"Light duties, but yeah. I'm on dispatch at the fire station, but I was just here after my shift to harass Robbie during his physiotherapy session. I didn't have time to change."

She smiled. "How is Robbie?"

"He's doing well." His gaze landed on her small round belly. "How are you feeling?"

"I'm good. I was here for my grant proposal. Second meeting, so it's looking good."

"That's great. We're really rooting for you at the fire station. It would be good for all of us."

"It would." She smiled; it was so easy to talk to him. She'd forgotten how easy. "I've missed you."

He reached out and took her hand. "I've missed you too."

"Why haven't you called?" she asked. "I thought we were going to tell Lucy."

"Lucy's been sick with tonsillitis and chicken pox. I didn't want you or the baby exposed to that."

"Oh! Why didn't you tell me?"

"I did. Of course, the night we briefly chatted you were very distracted…something about a research grant?" He smiled at her and her cheeks bloomed with heat.

Sandra chuckled. "Right. Now I remember. Oh, my God, I've been so annoyed at you lately, then, for no reason."

Kody's blue eyes sparkled and he laughed. "Sorry, but, see, I'm not as much of a jerk as you obviously thought I was."

"I guess not."

"How about we go tell Lucy now?"

Her heart skipped a beat. "Now? Are you certain?"

"Yeah, her school gets out soon. We can go and pick her up, get some soft serve and break the news to her." He glanced down at her belly. "She might pick up on the visual clues anyway. She is almost eight years old."

"Good point. Should I just follow you in my SUV to your place?"

Kody nodded. "Sounds good."

They walked out to the parking lot together and each went in their separate vehicles. Sandra followed Kody to his house and her heart was beating fast and her mind was going a mile a minute. She was worried that Lucy wouldn't react the way she hoped that she would.

She was worried that something was going to go wrong and even though Dr. Ohe said that her pregnancy was progressing normally,

Sandra still couldn't shake her fear. She still couldn't shake the feeling that she was about to lose everything.

It was one thing her losing everything, but she didn't want to hurt Lucy, who had lost so much already.

It was a quick drive to Kody's white stucco house from Rolling Creek. She left her briefcase with the letter in her car. Right now, she couldn't even focus on her genetics, she was so nervous about Lucy's reaction.

"You look like you're going to be sick. Are you okay?" Kody asked.

"I'm just… I'm *really* nervous about telling your daughter."

"It'll go well. Trust me."

She nodded, but it was hard to trust him. It was hard for her to even trust in herself. All that confidence she'd been feeling after her meeting with the board of directors was melting away. She wished she had a bit of that confidence right now.

"Come on, it'll be fine." Kody took her hand and they walked side by side toward Lucy's school. Her hand in his felt so right and it was nice to be able to enjoy an early-summer day with him.

They stood outside the gates of the school. There were other parents waiting. Groups of them in clusters, all talking.

There were parents waiting in cars and a crossing guard waiting for her charges. It was like something out of a movie.

This was what she'd always wanted. Of course, in San Diego it had been slightly different, and Alex had insisted that if they did have a baby they were going to hire a nanny.

"You're a surgeon and I'm a surgeon, Sandra. See sense—we have to keep working. I'm certainly not going to be a stay-at-home dad. We'll hire someone to take care of the child while we work. It's the only solution."

She had heard through the grapevine, before she'd left, that there was a top-of-the-line nanny lined up to take care of his child.

She wondered how that was going.

"Hey, do you think we should get a nanny?" she asked out of the blue.

Kody frowned. "A nanny? Why?"

"Well, we both work."

"Fair point, but we both get maternity and paternity leave. I say we think about a nanny when we have to go back to work."

"By then all the good ones will be gone."

Kody looked sideways. "Is this some kind of strange thing I don't know?"

"I guess because you had your sister and your in-laws helping you, you never really had to think about it."

"Jenny stayed home, but she wanted to stay home. She was doing online learning, so I guess, no, I never really had to think about it. Do you want to get a nanny?"

"If I go back to being a surgeon, yeah, I'm going to need one, especially as you might end up working the same shift as me and you said your sister, Sally, plans to go to medical school."

"Yeah. I guess that's something we'll have to look into." He sounded stressed and he was frowning.

"I'm sorry if I stressed you out. I didn't mean to. It just popped in my head."

"You are so weird sometimes. I've been meaning to tell you that." He winked at her.

"Look who's talking, sir, or should I refer to you as the purple streak?"

His lips pursed together, and she couldn't help but laugh.

"Remind me again to kill Megan when I see her," he muttered.

"I still want to see that blurry newspaper clipping."

"No. You don't."

The bell rang and all their talk about his streaking days ended as kids came pouring out of school, running toward their caregivers and the bus. Even though this was Sandra's first time to this school, it was easy to pick Lucy out of the mix. Her strawberry blond braid and brightly colored clothes were easy to pick out in the crowd.

"Dad!" Lucy jumped up and threw her arms around his waist. Kody still couldn't quite pick her up yet.

"I brought someone," Kody said. "She wanted to get some ice cream."

Lucy smiled up at her. "Dr. Sandra!"

"Hi, Lucy. Do you mind if I join you?"

Then Lucy's gaze fell on her belly. "Are you pregnant, Dr. Sandra?"

Sandra's pulse was thundering between her ears. "I am and that's something else we want to talk to you about."

Lucy nodded. "Okay, but can we get ice cream first?"

"Of course. We can walk to the Twisted Shack for just that and maybe after dinner we can go to the park."

Lucy gasped. "Can we go to the diner again? Last time Dr. Sandra was here we went to the diner!"

"Only because I burned dinner. I didn't this time, sucker!" he teased her gently and Lucy shook her head.

"I hope Aunt Sally cooked it," she muttered, and Sandra tried so hard to stifle her laughter.

"I can see where she gets her wit from."

"Oh, it's not all just me. Her mother had a good percentage of sarcasm in there," Kody said.

Even though Lucy was disappointed that they weren't going to the diner, she cheered right up the closer they got to the Twisted Shack, which served the soft ice cream that Sandra had been craving lately.

After they got their ice cream, they all sat down at the picnic tables outside the shack and enjoyed their treat. Sandra's stomach started fluttering like crazy, but she brushed it off as being hungry and ignored the fact that she was nervous.

"So, Lucy, you know how Dr. Sandra is having a baby, right?"

Lucy nodded. "Yeah."

"Well, the baby is also Daddy's. You're going to be a big sister," Kody said.

Lucy's eyes flew open and she had the biggest smile. "For real?"

"Yes," Sandra said. "I hope that's okay?"

"Yes!" Lucy said and she gave her a sideways hug. "I've always wanted to be a big sister. Is the baby a boy or a girl?"

"I don't know yet, love bug," Kody said. "But it's important to know that nothing changes between you and me."

"I know that, Dad, but this means our family is growing by two feet." She wrinkled up her face. "Well, I guess technically four feet."

Sandra was amused. "Four! I'm not having twins."

"I meant your feet, Dr. Sandra. You're a part of our family now too."

That simple statement filled Sandra's eyes with tears. She had never felt so accepted before, not since her adoptive parents, and they'd died when she was still in medical school. Her father didn't even get to walk her down the aisle. It was all so overwhelming, and it made her stomach go a bit wonky again.

"Are you okay, Dr. Sandra?" Lucy asked, concerned. "Are you sick?"

"Hmm, I might be, but I'm just so pleased that you're happy, Lucy." She shared a smile with Kody. They finished up their ice cream and then headed back to Kody's place. He held her hand again and it felt so right. They felt like a family.

Only you're not.

And she had to keep reminding herself of that fact. No matter how much she wanted it.

They got back to his place and Lucy went skipping off to her room, while Kody made dinner. They had a lovely dinner together and then spent the rest of the evening talking about the new baby. Lucy had a ton of questions for her and Sandra was more than happy to answer as many as she could.

Finally, it was bedtime for Lucy, and Sandra lingered while Kody put her to bed. When he came back, he went into the kitchen to clean up. Sandra followed him.

"You wouldn't have any of that ginger tea, would you?"

"Are you sick?" Kody asked, concerned. "You have been sort of off all night."

"I don't feel sick, but my stomach, it's been fluttering like I'm anxious. I mean, I was anxious, but now that Lucy is okay with it, I thought that it might go away, but my belly is racing."

Kody grinned. "I don't think it's nerves at all. Would you describe it like a butterfly?"

"Yeah. Why?"

"Sweetheart, that's the baby moving." Kody placed a hand on her stomach. "You're nineteen weeks—the baby is moving. This is called the quickening."

Sandra gasped and touched her belly. And when she did that, she felt the little zoom across her belly again and she started to cry.

"I've been so busy. I hadn't noticed. I thought it was nerves." A tear slid down her cheek. "The baby is moving!" Her baby was alive. Her baby was moving.

It was real.

It wasn't just some lovely dream.

Kody knelt beside her and held his hand on her belly too and then leaned in and whispered against her belly, something she couldn't quite make out because she was trying not to ugly cry.

"What did you say?" she asked.

"I told him or her that I love them. No matter what and I can't wait to see them."

"That's so nice," she sniffled.

"This is amazing, Sandra." Then he leaned up and he kissed her. Just as he had that night in the cabin. The night when she'd lost all her sense and taken a chance on something she'd thought would only be a memory right now.

And in this moment, knowing that her baby was thriving, she was glad that she had taken that chance, that moment with Kody.

The kiss deepened into something more, but she didn't care. She'd missed him. She'd thought about that night more often than she cared to admit and she would give anything to have it again.

To savor it.

His hands were in her hair and he tried to pull away, but she wanted him close. She didn't want this to end. She just wanted to feel connected to him, even if it was for the last time.

"No, I want this."

"Remember what happened the last time?" he teased huskily.

"I can't get pregnant again." She kissed him again, letting him know without words how much she wanted him. "Please, for tonight."

"I can't say no to you, no matter how much I know I should be strong." He scooped her up in his arms and carried her to his room.

Sandra was scared, but she wanted him. She just wanted to forget her worries, forget the sadness that was inside her. The loneliness that she felt. She wanted to be loved by him, one more time. They undressed quickly and then she lay on the bed, guiding him down to join her.

He sat down on the bed and lay down beside her, her back against his chest so that he didn't put pressure on her belly. He ran his hand across her skin, and she shivered in delight, her body wakening to his touch, as she always did when he touched her like that.

Kody tilted her chin so that she looked at him. Those brilliant blue eyes gazing deeply into hers, mesmerizing her. She'd forgotten how lost she got in his eyes.

He kissed her gently.

"Kody, I want this," she murmured.

"I know. So do I. I will be gentle, don't worry, but if anything feels uncomfortable stop me. Please."

She nodded, but she was still worried about the baby. She closed her eyes and reveled in the sensations he was stirring up inside her. Not that it took much—lately their one time together was all she could think about. She wanted him and she knew that sex during pregnancy was perfectly fine.

And she knew that Kody would be gentle with her. She wasn't worried about him.

She let out a sigh as his hands roved over her body. It sent delicious, electric sparks throughout her. She forgot everything else and just focused on the sensations and pleasure.

Right now, she just wanted to feel.

To taste passion one more time.

To have Kody possess her completely.

His mouth opened against hers as she kissed him, his kiss deepening, becoming more urgent. Never in her life had she wanted someone as badly as she wanted Kody. And she doubted there would ever be another like him. She doubted she'd ever feel this way about another man.

The kiss ended, leaving her breathless and her body hot, burning with need.

"I've missed you, Sandra," he whispered.

He wanted her as much as she wanted him.

"You're so beautiful." He kissed her neck and her back.

Her body thrummed with desire. His hand moved between her legs and she cried out, so sensitive to his touch. He helped her lift a leg over his legs so that he could enter her from behind and not put any pressure on her belly. As he entered her slowly it made her cry out in pleasure.

Their first time had been furious and frenzied; this time was slow and so delicious.

Her whole body tingled, and his hand cupped her breast as he began to move slowly.

Heady pleasure coursed through her. Hot, like fire.

Kody quickened his pace and she climaxed around him. He soon followed.

His hand relaxed and her body felt like melted goo. Her thighs quivered as the last of her orgasm moved through her system and she slowly lowered her leg, unable to hold it up any longer.

Kody rolled on his back and she curled up beside him, just listening to him breathe, while he drew lazy circles on her back with his fingers.

She didn't want to leave his bed even though she should.

"Do you want to stay the night?" he asked. "It's late and I would worry about you driving home."

"Sure. If you don't mind. I'm really tired."

He kissed her. "I don't mind. Just, don't get up in the morning until after I take Lucy to school. I don't want to confuse her. I've never had a woman stay here before."

"Of course." Sandra understood that.

She wanted to ask him what this meant, but she didn't dare, because she was so afraid that he'd reject her. That he wouldn't want her, because even though she tried to keep him out, she couldn't. Try as she might, she couldn't keep him at bay and she knew one thing was for certain after tonight, as she lay here listening to his heart beating and having him hold her so close—she was falling in love with him. Though she tried to fight it, she couldn't.

She'd never thought she would feel love again. Alex had broken her heart so completely and destroyed her trust and she was scared that Kody was dragging out these feelings that he was making her feel again.

She'd thought she'd done a good job hiding away her feelings. She'd thought she was better at compartmentalizing her life and her emotions, but just one night with Kody and she knew that she wasn't as good at that as she'd thought she was.

"You've gone quiet," he said gently.

"I'm a bit cold."

And that wasn't a lie. She *was* cold, and she didn't have any pajamas here. Although she didn't think she would need them anymore.

"You don't feel cold." He rolled over and dragged her into another kiss, which set her body on fire again.

She could get used to this.

Don't.

"Maybe you can keep me warm."

He smiled at her. "I can do that."

And he pulled her close, his hands on her body again, making her body sing when she'd thought it was spent. She realized then she would never get enough of Kody and that, when it came to him, she was a lost woman.

She was weak and not as strong as she'd thought she was.

Kody was her Achilles' heel and she was falling so madly in love with him, she realized there was no use fighting her feelings. She loved Kody and, though it scared her that he didn't and couldn't love her back, she couldn't help herself.

She only hoped that she wasn't right, because she was lost.

She was his and that scared her, but, for now, she was going to revel in her stolen moment of passion, even if it was for the last time.

CHAPTER ELEVEN

KODY WOKE UP to the feeling of something nudging him and he realized that he was spooning Sandra, his hand resting on her belly.

He smiled at the little movement from his baby. He wanted to do right by this little one and he would. He also wanted to do right by Sandra. He just wasn't sure how.

He felt the little nudge again. The baby reminded him of his weakness. And his weakness was Sandra. When they'd shared that night in the cabin, he'd sworn that nothing else would happen between them, he couldn't let it happen, but here he was. She was in his bed, pressed against him after another night of lovemaking, and he was so glad that she was here.

He didn't want to hurt her, because he loved her.

He was just terrified to reach out and take it. He felt as if he didn't deserve a second chance at happiness, and he wasn't sure that she wanted it.

Aren't you?

She stirred in her sleep, but he covered her back up and slipped out of bed without disturbing her. He got up and got ready for the morning. Lucy would be up soon, and he had to make sure that she got off to school.

Once she was off to school, he and Sandra could talk properly about what happened between them, and what was going to happen going forward with their child. And the thought of their child made him smile again.

He couldn't help but wonder what kind of person this new baby would grow up to be. There was this whole future that was yet to be determined and even if he and Sandra couldn't be together, he was going to be there for his child.

No matter what.

Yet his greatest fear was Sandra shutting him out or moving away.

Or falling for someone else?

The idea of her with another man made him angry, but he didn't know if she wanted him. He had no idea if she wanted to be saddled with a widower with a daughter and his late wife's memory constantly hovering over them.

It was only supposed to be one night, but, after that one night and last night, he knew it would never be enough.

And he wasn't sure how to reach out and take what he wanted. He still hadn't managed to tell Jenny's parents about Sandra. It terrified him.

Lucy got up without too much fuss. He didn't want her to see Sandra and he hoped that Sandra stayed in bed. Sandra knew that it wouldn't be good for Lucy to see her here, in the morning, coming from his room.

He walked Lucy to school and she was so excited to tell everyone that she was going to be a big sister. It made his stomach twist in knots, because he didn't want everyone to know.

He wasn't ready to tell everyone.

You've got to get over this.

And it was true. He had to.

Everyone was going to find out eventually. He just didn't know how he was going to break it to Myrtle and Ted. He felt as if he'd done the memory of their daughter wrong. He still couldn't shake the fact that he thought he'd wronged Jenny by falling in love with someone else.

He still loved Jenny, but he was in love with Sandra.

It was just, he couldn't have both.

He wasn't sure how to do that. And he didn't only want to give half of his heart to Sandra. She deserved so much more.

When he got back to his house, he saw Ted and Myrtle had pulled up outside, and immediately he went into panic mode.

"I thought we'd catch you on the way back from school," Myrtle said.

"Whose car is in the driveway?" Ted asked as he examined Sandra's car.

"A coworker," Kody said quickly. "She's starting up a new simulation lab that will benefit both first responders and surgeons during times of large-scale disasters. She's here to talk over the course."

"A bit early?" Myrtle asked.

"Well, you know doctors." Kody just hoped they believed his lie, because if the roles were reversed, he wouldn't.

"Ah, well, we'll leave you to it. Do you want us to pick Lucy up from school?" Myrtle asked.

"Yes. I mean, no... I mean, Sally is going to do it."

"Oh. Okay." Myrtle gave Kody a quick hug. "Then we'll leave you to your work. Don't forget about the flying lessons, now that you're healed up. We're here to babysit whenever."

"Thank you."

Kody opened the door for Myrtle, and Ted climbed in the driver's seat. He waved as they drove away, and Kody scrubbed a hand over his face.

He didn't know what to do.

* * *

Sandra had woken up to find that Kody was gone. He'd left a note to say that he'd taken Lucy to school. She knew to keep in the room until Lucy was off to school. They'd discussed it last night after it was decided she was sleeping over.

It was best for Lucy.

So when she found the note and didn't hear any sounds, she knew that it was safe to get up. She got dressed and made her way to the kitchen and on the way she noticed Kody talking to his in-laws out front. She heard the whole conversation as the living-room window was open.

She heard him lie about who she was.

Not exactly lie, but he didn't tell them about the baby or the fact that Lucy knew and that she'd actually spent the night, not just called by very early for a work meeting. Why was he so ashamed of her? Did she mean so little to him? What about when the baby came? Was he going to hide their child from Jenny's parents as he hid her?

Then she heard about flying lessons.

They'd bought him flying lessons and she remembered what he'd said before, when he'd been gearing up to become a pilot. Jenny had got pregnant with Lucy and he'd had to put his plans on hold.

Just as this pregnancy was once again delaying his dreams, and she felt awful for that.

She was holding him back.

I should've kept my distance. I should've kept my distance.

Well, the damage was done now. She was pregnant and he was involved, but she wasn't going to hold him back from what he wanted.

He came inside and was surprised to see her, or was he nervous that she'd heard the entire conversation? Which she had, but she wasn't going to let him know that.

"You're awake."

"I got your note, so I figured it was safe to come out. Lucy get off to school okay?" She hoped her voice wasn't trembling.

"She did." He rubbed the back of his neck. "Are you going to be heading back home now?"

"Yeah, I need a change of clothes and I'm

anxiously awaiting news about whether my research grant has been approved."

"I'll walk you to your car."

"Thanks." She didn't know what else to say. She was hurt, but she should've known. Why did she let her guard down when it came to matters of the heart?

"Are you okay?" he asked. She wanted to tell him yes, but she couldn't lie. He might, but she couldn't.

"No." She took a deep breath, her lip trembling. "Last night was a mistake."

He took a step back as if he'd been slapped. "Wait...what?"

They walked down the steps to her car. "I said last night was a..." but before she could finish what she was going to say they turned, both hearing an engine revving and then the squealing of tires. Sandra watched in horror as a sports car came roaring down the street and then she heard the train going by.

And as she watched in horror, she realized that the car was not going to stop for the train.

"Oh, my God," she whispered.

Kody's arm came around her as the low-slung vehicle hit the front of the train and was thrown into the air. The train's engine and the first two cars derailed and came crashing down on their sides.

There was an explosion and flames.

Kody covered her face and the only sound she could hear was the race of her pulse and metal grating on metal.

When the grinding came to a halt, there were lots of people out on the street, staring in abject horror at the carnage that was in front of them.

"If ever there was a time for your course, it would be now, Sandra," Kody said.

"I'll call the emergency services. There's a trauma kit in my car," she said. "Hurry!"

"Right." Kody opened her trunk and pulled out the trauma kit that she always carried with her. It was brand-new as she'd had to replace the one that was destroyed when her old SUV was washed away in Burl's Creek.

She called in for emergency services, but she wasn't the only one who had. Sandra could hear the distant wail of the fire trucks coming.

She slipped her purse in the car and then followed in Kody's footsteps to the accident scene. She couldn't do much in the way of lifting, but she could triage, she could bandage and she could help. She was not going to sit there and do nothing.

Kody was dragging those he could out of the wreckage and Sandra went to the sports car that was flipped on its side.

She pulled out her flashlight and looked in through the tinted windows. There was nothing to be done. She could tell the driver, a young man, was dead.

So she focused her attention on helping Kody. She could assess and triage those he brought out, until the rest of the first responders arrived.

She pulled out her equipment and began her quick assessments. She was going through the ABCs that she always did. Checking for airway and breathing, checking for consciousness and checking their pupils.

Superficial cuts and wounds could be handled later.

The first two people that Kody had managed to pull from the wreckage were gone. Their pupils were fixed and dilated. There was nothing more they could do.

She just had to keep moving on, through the line of carnage, and trying her best to help the first responders before they arrived.

It felt like an eternity, but soon she saw several ambulances heading down Kody's street toward them and she breathed a sigh of relief.

The first ambulance stopped, and Sally jumped out.

"Sandra? Are you okay?" Sally asked.

"I'm fine." Which was a lie—she was feeling a bit light-headed from the smoke. "There's a man over there who has a head injury and I suspect damage to his spine. Kody is working on more of the survivors that can't walk themselves out."

Sally motioned for her team to take over from Kody. He was still on restricted duty because of his broken ribs from his own traumatic accident.

Sandra was surprised that this situation wasn't bothering him more.

"What about the flipped car?" Sally asked, as she directed her team.

"Didn't stop at the crossing. It was hit and flipped. I checked and the driver is a young man and he's dead. There was brain matter coming out his ears and nose."

"We'll get a tarp up," Sally stated. "Stop people from taking and posting pictures before the police can notify the loved ones."

The police had arrived and were directing people back into their homes, while on the other side of the tracks the fire trucks were working on the fire.

The smoke was getting to Sandra and she felt woozy.

"Sandra, I think you need to sit down." Sally tried to help her, but Sandra shrugged her off.

"No, I can…" Everything went blurry and she felt as if she was going to pass out. It was as if her blood sugar was tanking. "I can help."

"I don't think you can." Sally steadied her. "Kody!"

Kody came running up and he smelled like fumes. "Sandra, are you okay?"

"I'm really faint."

"She's going pretty pale." Sally led her to the back of her rig. "I'm going to check your blood pressure, Sandra."

There was no use fighting. Sally was just as strong as Kody as they led her to the back of the rig. She sat down on the bumper, but it was no good.

Everything was turning into a pinpoint. Kody was getting farther and farther away.

"Sandra?"

"I'm…" was the last thing she said before she felt her knees give out, just as they had done when she'd first found out she was pregnant.

She was trying to tell Kody that she was about to faint, but as the world went black around her, she guessed that was a moot point.

Kody paced outside the exam room in the emergency department of Rolling Creek.

Sandra's blood pressure had dropped so low, it was scary.

It terrified him, and all he could think about was Jenny at the end of her life.

Please don't take Sandra. Please don't take the baby.

Sally helped him rush Sandra through and handed her off to Dr. Murdoch. Sally had to get back to the accident scene and, since the school had closed due to the accident, Myrtle and Ted went to get Lucy. Which he appreciated.

He was terrified and this was the reason why he'd never wanted to care about someone again. He didn't want to open his heart to anyone, but Sandra had wiggled her way in and he was angry.

He was angry that she'd managed to do that.

Dr. Ohe and Dr. Murdoch came out.

"How is she?" he asked nervously.

"She has gestational diabetes. Some women are more prone to it and if she had read that genetic report I gave to her yesterday she would've been on the lookout for it. She'll have to be on insulin until her pregnancy comes to term. She is also genetically predisposed to low blood pressure, so that's something else she'll have to keep an eye on."

"So the baby is okay?" Kody asked.

"Perfectly fine," Jocelyn said. "We're going to keep Sandra here overnight, just for observation."

"And she needs to stop overdoing it," Burt stated. "What she thought she was doing out there at that accident scene is beyond me."

"We witnessed it," Kody offered. "I guess she felt like she couldn't just stand there."

"Be that as it may, she needs to take it easy," Burt warned.

"Can I go in and see her?"

Burt nodded. "Let her know she's staying overnight."

Kody nodded and walked into the exam room. She looked so pale against the pillow. She was hooked up to an IV and there were dark circles under her eyes.

It was scary to see her like this.

I can't do this.

It was just bringing back too many memories of Jenny, lying there in the last moments of her life, and him on his knees begging her to fight harder. Now Sandra was lying there, ill, and it scared him. He couldn't lose her or the baby. He couldn't risk it all again.

She opened her eyes. "I overdid it."

"That's not quite it," he said quietly. "Why didn't you tell me your genetic report came in? Diabetes is indicated in your genetic makeup, as is low blood pressure."

"I got the report yesterday and then ran into you and I forgot all about it."

"Why don't you want to know about your past?" he asked.

"Why are you so upset?" she asked, confused. "I'm okay."

"Not if you keep overdoing it. You shouldn't have got involved in that accident."

She frowned. "What was I supposed to do? Sit there?"

"Yes!" Kody snapped. "You could've lost the baby."

"I didn't. The baby is fine."

Kody scrubbed a hand over his face. "You need to face your past. I get that you had great adoptive parents, but you have to find out about your past. If not for you, then for our baby. You have to face this fear."

She pursed her lips together. "You're one to talk."

"What're you talking about?" he asked.

"Don't lie to me."

"I'm not lying to you. I really don't know what you're talking about."

"Myrtle and Ted. They don't know about me, do they? I heard your conversation this morning and about the flying lessons."

His blood ran cold and he knew then she'd overheard the conversation that he was worried that she'd overheard.

He'd tried to tell them. He had, but he couldn't and he hated lying to Sandra about it, especially when he kept promising that he was going to tell them.

"They were a gift."

"That still doesn't explain why you won't tell them. Do I embarrass you? I am an adopted child with no roots."

"Pardon?" Kody asked. "I'm not embarrassed."

"So why don't you tell them? Why do you lie to me and them?"

"Is this why you were trying to blow me off this morning?" he asked.

"It was a mistake. All of it."

"It wasn't!" he snapped.

"Then tell Jenny's parents about me."

"It's complicated."

Sandra sighed. "They're eventually going to find out. They probably already know—you think that Lucy can hide that secret well?"

"It's my business," he snapped. "I'm not the only one holding back. You've kept everyone out because you're afraid of having a family. You're afraid of happiness and you can't keep blaming that on your ex-husband."

It was a low blow, but he felt as if he was backed into a corner. He'd been terrified that she was hurt or had lost the baby. He was angry at himself that he was too scared to move forward. That he was paralyzed with fear at the prospect of losing her.

"My ex-husband lied to me. Just like you are. He didn't want kids that weren't his own blood. You know that. I wasn't good enough for him. He wanted a biological family and I couldn't give that to him. He made me feel worthless. He took away all of my confidence. It's why I keep my distance from people and it's why I should've trusted my first instincts and kept my distance from you!" Tears were rolling down her cheeks.

There was nothing more to say. Not right now. He was so confused.

"I think I'd better go." He turned to leave.

He'd hurt her because he was too scared about taking another chance at happiness. He didn't deserve to even think about having a second chance at happiness. He'd had it once and he was greedy thinking that he could have it again.

And now he'd blown that chance too. All because he was too afraid about the risk to his heart again. Lucy, Myrtle and Ted were just excuses. It was him. He was afraid and he wouldn't admit it.

CHAPTER TWELVE

"I'M SURE HE didn't mean those things," Megan said gently.

"I know," Sandra replied. "And he's right. I endangered the baby because I had to help."

"You're a doctor—of course you had to help. The baby is fine." Megan squeezed her hand.

Sandra sighed. "I am scared."

"Of what?" Megan asked.

Sandra couldn't put it into words. She was scared that she'd fallen in love with Kody and Lucy. She was scared of losing them both.

She was scared that they wouldn't want her in their lives.

She was scared of being rejected again. She'd been rejected her whole life. Her birth parents didn't want her and neither did Alex in the end.

People were constantly leaving her and, as much as she wanted a family, as much as she wanted Kody and loved him, she was terrified of losing him. She was terrified that he was going to walk out of her life, so she'd helped push him out, but she knew that he was afraid too and she didn't know how to reach him.

She didn't know if there was room in his heart for anyone but his late wife.

"I'll check on you later," Megan said. "You try to rest."

"I'll try."

Megan left and Sandra grabbed her briefcase. She pulled out the genetic report that she'd shoved in there. She opened it up and saw that low blood pressure and anemia were two things she'd inherited.

Diabetes was also indicated.

She learned that she was 70 percent Dutch and 30 percent French, which made her smile. The Dutch thing was unexpected, but it was neat to see on the map where her ancestors were from. Also, a common surname that seemed to pop up was Rutant.

It was such a French surname compared to the surname of her adoptive parents, which was decidedly Scottish, but one thing it did, she thought, staring at her genetic report and reading about the DNA sequences that made up her, was give her roots. It gave her a sense of belonging and it was something she could share with her baby.

She knew something about where she came from. The next step was to check out that letter about her adoption record. Hopefully, they'd been able to contact her parents and see if they were willing to tell her more.

But as Kody always said, she was going to take it one day at a time.

She hoped that Kody would come back so she could clear the air. She wanted to move forward. She wanted him to know that she wasn't going to hold him back and if he wasn't ready for a relationship, she understood, but she was going to tell him how she felt.

She was tired of hiding who she was.

She was tired of hiding behind the walls she'd built. It was lonely there. She was afraid to take a chance, but she was ready to put Alex and everything behind her.

She was ready to go forward into the future. Whatever that might be.

Kody took a deep breath and headed up the steps to his in-laws'. He was pretty sure that Lucy had probably already told them that she was going to be a big sister, and he owed it to Ted and Myrtle to tell them about Sandra.

He owed it to Jenny and he owed it to Sandra and most of all he owed it to himself.

In order to move forward he had to make room in his heart for Sandra. If she would have him. If she ever forgave him. He'd taken out his fear on her. When he'd seen her collapse, he'd been terrified of losing her and the baby.

He wasn't sure Sandra could ever forgive him.

And if she didn't, he'd still be there for her, for the baby. The most important thing to do now was tell Myrtle and Ted about Sandra.

And it wasn't that he had to make room in his heart for Sandra—he already had. Jenny had wanted him to move on, but he knew that it would be hard for her parents and he didn't relish telling them and letting them down.

If he didn't really want to be with her, he wouldn't have fallen for her the way he did. Others had tried to set him up on dates since Jenny had died, but none of those dates had ever led anywhere.

With Sandra, he had been sucked in and he loved her.

He wanted to be a family with her, Lucy and the new baby. As long as he hadn't ruined everything. And if he did ruin something, he was going to spend as long as he could making it right.

He just hoped that Myrtle and Ted understood.

When he walked into their home they were sitting in their living room and he could hear Lucy in their den, watching television. She had her headphones on and she hadn't noticed him, which was fine, because he didn't want her to interrupt.

"So," Myrtle started, breaking the ice. "Lucy tells us there's a baby?"

"Yeah, um… Dr. Sandra Fraser. We had a night together a few months ago and she's pregnant."

"Do you love her?" Ted asked point-blank.

"I do. I didn't want to. I want you to both know that. I loved Jenny so much, but I've fallen in love with Sandra and I'm hoping she loves me and Lucy too. Well, I know that she loves Lucy."

Myrtle smiled gently. "We know that you loved Jenny. You took care of her, you stepped up when she was so sick and you've done everything to keep her memory alive for us all, but, Kody, we never expected you to stay celibate for the rest of your life, only living to mourn our Jenny."

"I'll always mourn Jenny," Kody said quickly. "She wanted me to move on…but I could never bring myself to do it. I just couldn't move on."

"Because you hadn't found the right person," Ted said. "Son, we know. We understand. You could've talked to us about this. We love our daughter and it pains us every day that she's not here, but she's not and you can't stop living because of that."

Kody shook his head. "Sally has told me the same."

Myrtle smiled and stood up, giving him a hug. "You have our blessing, for what it's worth, and we're happy and thrilled about the baby. We hope that we can be a part of this new baby's life too."

Kody smiled and squeezed Myrtle's shoulder in a half-hug. "Of course! My parents are far away and Sandra doesn't have parents. Her adoptive parents were older and died some time ago. Other than me and Lucy, she's been alone."

Tears welled up in his mother-in-law's eyes. "It's like Jenny sent her to us, then. We love you, Kody, and we'll love this new baby too. And, please, bring Sandra by so that we can let her know that she's already a part of our family."

Kody got choked up. "You don't know how much this means to me."

Ted nodded. "You don't know how much

it means to Myrtle and me that you included us in your life, that you didn't shut us out."

"I would never shut you guys out, but we're probably going to be moving out of our little house in the city—that's if Sandra takes me back. Her house outside the city is a lot larger, but, then again, she may not want to see me anytime soon. We had a bit of a blowout. She overdid it at the accident scene and fainted and…we lost our tempers."

"I'm sure she'll forgive you," Myrtle said.

"I hurt her badly."

"Then grovel, son. Grovel." Ted winked. "Every couple fights. I knew you and Jenny had a few doozies. Things always work themselves out, especially when love is involved. You do love Sandra, don't you?"

"I do. I never thought that I would love someone like this again and it's not like my heart has closed off to Jenny, but it's like it's expanded. I guess the same way a parent equally loves all their children just the same."

Myrtle nodded. "Go to her and make it right."

Kody kissed Myrtle on the top of the head.

"Can you guys keep Lucy for the night? Sandra's in for observation and I want to stay with her."

"Of course," said Ted. "Now, go make it right."

"Jewelry helps," Myrtle teased.

Kody laughed. He wasn't quite ready to propose, but he wanted to set everything right. He was going to make sure that Sandra knew how he felt and that he wanted to be with her. He wanted to raise their child together. He wanted to be a family.

Sandra was very tempted to turn Kody away when he showed up to her room up on the maternity floor, but she wasn't as angry as she had been when they'd fought earlier, and she was glad that he'd come back. She hadn't been sure that he would.

She was very emotional when he walked in the door with a big teddy bear.

"They wouldn't let me bring flowers up, or balloons, and I didn't think you really wanted a basket of fake flowers, so I brought this. Although, Myrtle suggested jewelry."

She was stunned. "You talked to your in-laws?"

"I did and they're happy and want you to know that if you'll have them, they would like to be part of our family."

Tears stung her eyes. "I'd like that. Wait, what do you mean, our family?"

"Sandra, I've been a fool. I've been carrying around this guilt because I was falling in love with you. I felt like I was betraying Jenny. I felt like all I deserved was one love in my life and I felt like you deserved more than half a heart, but the longer I've got to know you, the more I realized that it's simply not true."

"What?" she asked quietly.

"It's not half-hearted. My heart just expanded and you're in there, with Jenny. The both of you, and I love you. Try as I might, you wiggled your way in there and I fell in love with you. You're not holding me back. Sure, my life didn't go exactly as I planned, but when does life ever go as planned?"

"Right," she said, tears streaming down her face. "So you're saying you love me?"

"I do. I love you and I'm so sorry for our fight. It was a petty thing and I was scared. You don't understand how scared I was when I saw you lying there, unconscious and your blood pressure tanking. It brought back all those nightmarish memories of Jenny dying. I couldn't lose you and the baby. I just couldn't, so I acted cowardly. I'm sorry." He took her hand and kissed it.

Sandra reached out and touched his face. "I love you too. And you're right, I've been afraid too."

"You're one of the strongest women I know."

"Perhaps, but I was scared. I was scared of opening my heart again. I lost so much, and so many people in my life have left me. I was left in a bathroom, in a high school here in Austin. I was fortunate to be adopted, but my adoptive parents died within a year of each other and left me alone and then Alex, the first man I loved, left me. I couldn't even stay pregnant. So, everyone left and I just got so used to being alone. You weren't the only one pushing the other away, I was doing the same and, for that, I'm sorry. I love you, Kody. I love Lucy and I want to try and make this work. I want to be a family. If you'll take a chance on someone who gets rejected an awful lot."

Kody smiled. "Your ex-husband was a fool. I'll never leave you, Sandra. I think that Jenny sent you to me and Lucy, because you're exactly who we needed in our life."

She cried then and he climbed into the bed beside her and touched her belly.

"I love you both, but you have to promise me something."

"What's that?"

"Don't scare me like that again."

"I won't. So, what happens next?" she asked nervously, leaning her head against him.

"I don't know. I don't know where this is going yet, but all I know is I want you by my side. I want you in Lucy's life. I just want all of you and I'm scared to take these steps too. The uncertainty of it all is thrilling and scary."

She reached up and kissed him. "We'll do

what you told me when I was anxious about being pregnant and staying pregnant."

"What's that?" he asked.

"One day at a time. We'll take it one day at a time. That's all we can do."

He chuckled and pulled her closer. "I love you, Sandra Fraser."

"I love you too, Mr. Davis."

He laughed, because that was a reminder of the old Sandra. He used to dread her icy demeanor when he came into the emergency room and had to deal with her, but he'd also been attracted to her. Now he realized painfully that his first assessment of her had been so wrong. She was icy to protect her heart, just as he was aloof to others to keep his heart protected, but now he was glad that the walls they'd both built to keep themselves safe had come crashing down.

Now they could take those individual bricks that they guarded their hearts with and build a solid foundation to stand on.

A foundation where they could stand together. It would be him, Sandra, Lucy and the new baby. And behind them would be the memory of those they'd loved and lost. Ahead of them would be the family of their own choosing and, most of all, they would be united by love.

They were in this together.

United as one family.

Forever.

And that was exactly the way he wanted it, even if he'd never believed it would be possible to feel this way again. He was glad that he'd been proven wrong.

And as Sandra settled in beside him, he sighed in contentment. No, he couldn't completely predict the future, but he was going to make sure that they stayed together. He wasn't going to let this gift from his guardian angel go.

He was in it for the long haul.

He was Sandra's forever.

"I love you," he whispered again.

"Ditto," she said, sounding sleepy. "Now, when are you and Lucy going to move to my ranch? Because I'm certainly not moving into that tiny house in the city."

"Now who's jumping the gun? Remember what you said."

"Right. One day at a time."

Yes. One day at a time. Forever.

EPILOGUE

One and a half years later

SANDRA COULD HEAR Lucy laughing hysterically through the open window, and she could also hear the squeals of Lucy's little sister, Samantha.

She peeked out the front window of her house and saw that Lucy was running around the big picnic blanket that Kody and Samantha were lounging on.

Sandra laughed. She had no idea what was so funny to Samantha, but it was cute all the same. And all she could do was stand there and watch them. Just for a moment.

One year ago, she'd never thought that she would be here.

That she would have this family.

That she would be getting married today. Although, it wasn't going to be a fancy service. It was just going to be their relatives gathering to see her and Kody married by an officiant in their front yard, with their daughters by their side.

Myrtle and Ted, Sally, Ross and the rest of her and Kody's family from North Carolina. Even Sandra's own biological father, John, would be here. Just before she'd given birth to Samantha she had opened her adoption record and reached out. Her biological father had responded and each day they built a relationship.

He'd had no idea that she existed, and he had been alone too.

Sandra had never heard from her biological mother, but that was okay. Maybe one day. For now, she was happy. She'd gone from being completely alone to having what she always wanted. A family.

Her big ranch that she'd bought because it was dilapidated and cheap was now a real family home. The rooms were filled, and she was no longer lonely.

The back meadow was being converted into a landing strip so that Kody could continue his flying lessons. After the sale of his house in Austin, he'd bought himself a small plane. That way, he could get air time, while still being close to the family.

It might not be Alaska, but at least he was still living a part of his original dream.

He was a pilot.

And Sandra was now the director of Rolling Creek's newest simulation lab, and her course on triaging and surgery in the field for large-scale natural disasters was one of the most renowned in the Southern states.

Other cities and hospitals were sending their doctors and their first responders to learn from her. There were times when she missed the emergency department and the operating room, but with this project there were no more night shifts and she was able to spend more time with her children.

Lucy might not be biologically hers, but she still loved her as her own. Lucy was her daughter but Sandra would never let Jenny's memory fade.

She stepped outside.

"I hope that you three are keeping clean.

The guests will be arriving soon," she scolded gently.

"We're keeping clean." Kody stood up, picking up Samantha and giving her a gentle toss in the air. "Aren't we?"

Samantha just squealed and Kody set her down in her playpen, pulling the sunshade over it. Lucy had retreated to the blanket to play with her dolls and Kody came over to see Sandra. He wrapped his arms around her and gave her a kiss on the top of her head, as he always did.

"How are you feeling today? Still tired from all the wedding prep?"

"Um, sort of," she said slyly. "I have something to tell you."

"Oh, do I want to hear this?"

"You might." She couldn't stop smiling, because she'd never thought Samantha would happen and she had been just as shocked when she'd received the call from Jocelyn about her lab results.

"What is it?"

"I'm pregnant again. Jocelyn called me this morning. I'm six weeks gone already."

Kody's eyes widened. "You are? So soon?"

"I know. Samantha is almost a year old, and I didn't think that I would get pregnant again, but I went for my routine checkup and told her I was feeling tired. I thought it had to do with opening up the simulation lab's new addition and all the work I've been doing. I certainly haven't had the same symptoms I did when I was pregnant with Samantha."

Kody shook his head. "I'm so…"

"What? Are you happy?"

"Of course I am." He pulled her close and kissed her. "Of course. I think I can't quite believe it myself. For so long I thought that Lucy would be my only child. I always wanted a big family, but until I met you, I thought that wasn't in the cards for me. And then Samantha came along and we were so lucky to have her, I just never expected a third."

"Well, maybe this time you'll finally get a boy, so you're not so outnumbered by all these girls," Sandra teased.

Kody laughed. "I don't mind being out-numbered by all these girls. I'm so happy that you're in my life. I'm so happy that you love Lucy as much as Jenny did."

"I'm so happy that Jenny gave me such a wonderful daughter."

He kissed her again.

"Thank you for opening up your heart for me," she whispered. "I love you."

"I love you too." He kissed her one more time. "It's a good thing you agreed to marry me. It's about time I made an honest woman out of you."

She gasped and hit him. "How very sexist of you."

"Sorry." He chuckled. "I couldn't help it."

"So are we going to wait forever to tell Lucy about the prospect of another baby or are we going to actually tell her when the first trimester is over?"

"Why don't we tell her now?" Kody offered.

"What if something happens?" Sandra asked.

"We'll take that one day at a time." He reached down and touched her belly. "Baby steps, remember?"

She placed her hands over the top of his and nodded. "Baby steps."

They walked hand in hand to the blanket where Lucy was playing and sat down next to her to tell her that soon there would be two babies.

That their family was growing by two more feet.

* * * * *

LET'S TALK

Romance

For exclusive extracts, competitions
and special offers, find us online:

f facebook.com/millsandboon

⊙ @millsandboonuk

🐦 @millsandboon

Or get in touch on 0844 844 1351*

For all the latest titles coming soon,
visit millsandboon.co.uk/nextmonth